Surviving the Storm

Chapter 1

"Yeah Jenna, I know you are right, I need to get out there and start dating again. I am just so tired of it, I certainly don't want to die knowing that my baby daddy is the last man I slept with, that would be a total waste, but internet dating? It seems so pathetic"

"Um I am not positive it's politically correct for a 37-year-old white woman to refer to her ex as her baby daddy. I think sperm donor is probably a better description but yeah you need to start dating again, you aren't getting any younger and you deserve to have someone in your life. The internet is a good way to weed out the bottom feeders."

Liz Bartlett and Jenna Johnson had been friends for over 17 years. They had met, both at the age of twenty in travel school, a trade school to train people how to be travel agents, a service that would pretty much become obsolete before they had their certificates of completion in hand. Neither ever admitted the travel school debacle publicly to anyone. They usually preferred telling people who asked that they met in prison, or AA. The unlikely duo of Liz, the girlie girl who stood 5 foot 4 inches tall with brown hair and blonde highlights that were always done to perfection. Her nails perfectly manicured and lip gloss always in place, she loved being a girl and looking the part. You would not ever see Liz Bartlett slumming around in old sweats and a dirty t shirt, it just was not who she was. She liked to feel pretty, and she needed to be noticed when she walked into a room. She was not a stunning beauty, but she was attractive, that combined with her midwestern charm and outgoing personality usually meant she owned every room she entered. Jenna, her best friend the lesbian was Liz's polar opposite in this area, she was a 6-foot-tall, tomboy of a woman who wore her hair very short. She generally because of her size found men's clothes to be more comfortable, her hair, blonde and spiked along with the wallet in her back pocket sometimes had her mistaken for being a man. In spite of these basic differences they had far more in common than any outsider would recognize, and they formed a friendship that could be compared to the greatest friendships of all time. Lucy and Ethel, Laverne and Shirley, Burt and Ernie, and Liz and Jenna. They share, a quick wit and dry sense of humor, a level of intelligence superior to most of the free world, and an intense loyalty that promised a lifelong friendship. They were completely open with each other and didn't have to worry about social graces, they counted on each other for honesty, corruptibility and humor. Everyone knew if you asked either of them to keep a secret it went without saying that they would tell no one but each other. "Just join one of those online interracial dating sites and sit back and let it happen, you know that is all you have to do. Black men love you and you love black men so there is no point in wasting your time looking anywhere else because you won't give any other man a second glance," Jenna said as though it was just matter of fact.

"I might." Liz did not even believe her own words.

"Yeah, right" Jenna pulled the phone back looking at the receiver. "Let's try and remember who you are talking to shall we?"

"Ok, good point" Liz grinned to herself knowing her best friend was exactly right.

"Now get off my phone, the new season of Biggest Loser is about to start, call me on commercial so we can decide who we love and who we hate"

"Deal Pal, I will call you in 15, I should have a screen name by then" They had always called each other "Pal" no one really remembered how it started, or even noticed it anymore but the world around them knew exactly who the other was referring to when they said "Pal".

Liz hung up the phone turned on Biggest Loser and opened her laptop. She searched interracial dating and was pleasantly surprised to find several sites that seemed decent. She decided on the first one she came to because it was cheap. First, she needed a screen name which would allow every man browsing to know exactly what she wanted and didn't want. **Lookin4myblkman** that was pretty straight forward and should rule out what she wasn't looking for Liz thought. She kind of wanted to have her screen name be something like **Dontaskmeforagreencard** or **NoIdontsendnakedpics** but it seemed better to just be honest without being too negative. Liz thought carefully about what to say in her profile. "Single mom of one son who owns her own home." No that might draw a man who is looking for a woman to support him. Shoot this was going to be harder than she thought.

"37-year-old SWF, mom of one son, independent, humorous, just putting her toes in the water. Looking for an intelligent, goal oriented, black man. Men with gold teeth or an aversion to a wooden leg need not apply"

It sounded good to Liz, it didn't say too much but showed she had a sense of humor. Liz was not the kind of woman who felt like she would need to go looking for a man. She remembers her grandmother telling her more than once "If a man is interested, he will let you know". There are certain small pieces of wisdom you can count on from an older woman. Men haven't changed in a million years so Liz knew if her grandmother told her something about men whether she wanted to hear it or not it was certainly going to prove itself true. Liz paid her $9.99 to join for a month and hit submit. The deed was done, her face was out there on a dating site for the world to see. "Lord, what have I done?" Liz whispered to herself. She did not feel the need to go trolling through the men on the site, she knew they would come to her. She wasn't a raving beauty, but she was cute, and men were always drawn to her, she had charisma and confidence and she had learned in her thirty-seven years of life these were qualities that would get a girl much further than just her good looks. Liz then deleted her Internet history, as this wasn't information, she wanted to share with her 12-year-old son, Jackson. Jackson had her wit and charm along with his father's eyes. He would never have a problem with women, that was obvious before he could walk, and frankly scared the hell out of Liz. One thing was for sure, he would probably never have to internet date. Liz shut down her computer and tuned into Biggest Loser. She and Jenna would call each other every commercial to talk about strategy, game play, and how much they loved the trainer and her butt kicking abilities. It's so much easier to sit on the couch with a box of Twinkies and watch other people suffer the wrath of trainers from hell. The phone rang at the first break.

"Ok I love, love, love the purple team, but wow those are some big girls!" They didn't waste the 2.7 minutes of commercial time with niceties like "hello".

"I'm with ya, I can tell already I am not going to like the red team at all, I think the guy has a cock eye." Liz always paid strict attention to detail.

"This isn't the Miss America Pageant, who cares if he has a cock eye?" Jenna rolled her eyes and stared at the receiver.

"Well," Liz began, "by week three you are going to be obsessed with the creepy, cock eye and blogging for him to go home, ok it's back on talk to you shortly." The phone clicked off.

Now Liz had planted the seed and Jenna would be staring at the guy on the red team searching for the cock eye.

This was their routine three nights a week. Although they talked every day, three nights a week they kind of watched television together. They would watch their favorite programs and call each other on commercial to talk about it. Now that Jenna had a live-in girlfriend for the first time in ten years they didn't talk quite as much as they used to. Liz was happy for her, although sometimes she kind of missed having her friend around a little more. That was one of the weird things about having a best friend who is a lesbian, you couldn't just go to lunch like girls do because the girlfriend is a girl too, so she is included in everything. It was nice because whenever Jenna had a new girlfriend, Liz inherited a new friend. Liz was truly happy Jenna found someone, but the downside was that if they broke up Liz was expected to forfeit any friendships she developed with Jenna's girlfriends, that was the just how it went, and everyone seemed to know that going in. Overall Marybeth, Jenna's girlfriend, was a sweet woman, good for Jenna and at least now people would stop assuming Liz was her undercover girlfriend.

After Jackson finished his homework and headed off to bed Liz took her laptop and did the same. Twenty-six new emails all from the dating site in one hour! Liz was shocked. "Well, time to weed out the bottom feeders" Liz said to herself. She knew she needed to be a bit more positive, but at thirty-seven and having kissed hundreds of frogs, hope was running out. The first email was from screen name **BigPoppa**, he was fifty-six years old and had braids, Liz shook her head and quickly hit delete. Email number two was from **NineInchNailU**, no reason to even open that one, delete. Email number three was from **BigBalla** a 22 year old boy in his college basketball uniform, it said "Wow you are beautiful, I play ball at the University Of Michigan, I don't have a car but since you live here in Ann Arbor that won't be a problem, I share a dorm room with two other guys, do you have your own place? Looking forward to hearing from you, Shaun"

Liz had to respond "Shaun, thank you so much but you are too young for me and for dating sites. Go out and ride your bike and play with your friends or I am going to have to call your mother and tell her what you have been up to! Have a great night, Liz. P.S. No I don't have my own place, I have a roommate too, it's my twelve-year-old son."

Most of the emails were pretty similar, Liz let out an exasperated sigh. The decent ones all seemed to be a thousand miles away from her home town of Ann Arbor, Michigan. A long-distance relationship was not something she was even slightly interested in. Liz remembered a coworker who had been having a long-distance affair with this man she met on the Internet. They would talk on the phone for hours and meet every month or two at a hotel. He even took her on a few trips, and then one day she got a call from his wife. No thanks she thought, long distance relationships were definitely something she wanted to avoid at this stage of the game. Finally, Liz opened email number twenty-one from **OhMyGoodness.** It said, "Hello Beautiful, my name is Antoinne, I am 32 years old, I live in the Ann Arbor area. If you read my profile and find that you may be interested, please email me back. Have a great night." Liz scrolled his stats. Single, never married, Master's Degree, no kids. Clean cut, shaved bald, wearing a suit. He wasn't shirtless, which put him one up on half the profiles she saw. No spelling mistakes or bad grammar in his description, wow he was two for two! Ok, this guy might be ok. She isn't thrilled he is five years younger, but five years isn't a big deal, right? Liz replied, "Hi Antoinne thanks for the email. My name is Liz. I have one son he is 12 going on 20, when I am not at his football games, wrestling tournaments, or track meets I am generally running him to a friend's house, lol. Glad you weren't intimidated by my wooden leg, you should know I'm a real freak when I take it off!" Liz thought it was best to end with a little humor and clicked send. A few minutes later there was a response from Antoinne, "I'm not scared! Wooden legs are sexy, lol. You are cute, and you have a good sense of humor, I like that. Can I have your email address or phone number so we can get to know each other?"

Panic rose in Liz's throat. Phone number? So soon? Was she really ready to pick herself up by her bootstraps and move forward? Leave that jerk she had been with on and off for the past fifteen years alone, and really, truly move forward? The answer in her gut was a resounding YES! Liz needed to be completely done with this lying, cheating man who had never made her or their son a priority in his life. She knew she hadn't loved him in a long time but thought she owed it to their son, Jackson, to keep trying. He deserved a real family. She felt guilty for being a single mom. She desperately wanted Jackson's dad to take a real interest in him and in his life but that wasn't going to happen. He came around to see him only when he thought he could get Liz into bed. If she wasn't part of the package, then he wasn't going to be there. The problem was that he didn't want to commit to Liz and Jackson to be a family, he was running all over town playing house with God knows how many women. Liz didn't want to be with this man. He wasn't good for her, or for Jackson and the sooner she was able to move on once and for all, the better off they would all be. He brought out the very worst in Liz. He made her angry and suspicious and she found herself doing and saying things to him she never thought she was capable of, yes it was best for all of them if they went their separate ways. More than anything Liz wanted to meet a man who would love her and Jackson and fill the hole in her little boy's heart that ached for a father. She knew those were mighty big shoes for any man to fill and realistically it probably would not happen. The guilt of not giving her perfect little boy an amazing dad kept her awake at night and changed the way she parented. She struggled to be both mom and dad and when she failed, she over compensated and spoiled him rotten because she felt like such a failure.

Liz responded to Antoinne "Well since I don't see your mugshot on the America's Most Wanted website, I guess it's ok for you to call me" Liz typed in her cell phone number and clicked send. "What did I just do?" Liz asked to no one in particular. "I just gave my phone number to a stranger who may very well be a serial killer." she thought. Liz pictured the look on her parents face when they got the call, "Your daughter was on a date with a serial killer she picked up on the Internet. No, she isn't dead, but she will wish she was, the seven o'clock news is covering the story and there are no less than fifty reporters in front of your home right now. They all wonder if you raised her to be the kind of girl who picks up strange black men on the Internet and then agrees to go out with them." Oh yes that would certainly be a proud moment for everyone. Suddenly the phone rang, it was a number she didn't recognize, Liz knew it was him. She stared at it wondering if she should really answer it or if maybe she should just ignore it and hope he goes away. "Oh, why not?" Liz said to herself and picked up the phone. "Hello" she said in her sweetest voice.

"May I speak with Liz please?" the deep, sexy voice on the other side asked.

"Speaking" Liz's heart was pounding so loud she was worried he could hear it through the phone.

"Hey, it's Antoinne, how are you?"

"I'm great, Antoinne, how about you?" Liz replied.

"Good, I am just watching the basketball game, do you like basketball?"

"Actually, I love basketball, I just turned the game on myself. I think the Pistons have a great shot of going all the way this year"

"Yeah, me too" Antoinne responded. "You have a nice voice"

"Thank you, so do you"

The conversation continued for the next forty minutes. It flowed with ease. He impressed her with his intelligence and drive. Not many men his age were able to accomplish the things he had accomplished. He drove a new BMW, owned his own company and several rental properties, this all showed her his drive and ambition, a quality Liz found extremely sexy. His love of real estate is something they shared, and Liz was excited to discuss this with him more. It was an interest of hers that she hadn't really had time to explore fully and she couldn't wait to pick his brain and learn more about it. He owned several rental properties and employed two contracting teams to flip houses. He had just had plans drawn up to build a new five thousand square foot house. Liz loved real estate, she was a real estate show junkie and often surfed the real estate sites for great bargains. House hunting was the ultimate shopping experience, and she didn't have to try on anything. The conversation couldn't be going better, Liz thought. This guy sounded great. She found herself very interested in seeing his house plans. "Maybe you can show me your blueprints sometime," Liz casually dropped the hint that she would be interested in seeing him in person.

"Yeah, I will bring them out when I see you," he answered right on cue. She knew she needed to be the one to end the conversation first, it was in every rule book ever written about dating. "Well I have really enjoyed talking to you, but it's getting late and I should be getting to bed" Liz said, although she could have stayed up all night talking to him, she was trying to start out right for a change.

"Ok sexy, can I call you tomorrow?" Antoinne replied.

"I would like that" Liz said in her best pillow talk voice.

"Goodnight"

"Goodnight Sweetie" He replied, and she waited to hear him disconnect.

Liz stared at ceiling. This was the first time in a long time she felt a spark of interest in a guy. No kids, which means no exes to deal with. He is smart and educated, and this is probably too good to be true she thought. She laid there wondering what was wrong with him. Did he hit women? Did he have herpes? Or worse, what if he is only 5'3" tall? Maybe he is a premature ejaculator. Maybe his penis is an inch long. Maybe he is all of the above which she figured was the most likely. Liz was laying there thinking horrible thoughts about what was to come, working herself into a full-blown anxiety attack when the ding of her cell phone alerted her to a new text message. "Hey, it's Antoinne, I think we are really going to hit it off. Sweet dreams" Liz found herself grinning like a teenager. She typed back "Sweet dreams to you too Sunshine".

"Ok Liz" she often talked out loud to herself, "You need to get a grip. This may just be a great guy who doesn't wear white socks with a cheap suit. Maybe, just maybe, his breath won't make you throw up in your mouth a little." She was going to give herself a good pep talk if it killed her. "Well it's not like you haven't been on a million crappy dates in your life old girl, what is one more? Lord, I really need to stop talking to myself all the time." Liz rolled herself around a pillow, pulled up her blanket and decided to put the whole thing out of her mind until tomorrow. After all, there was still a good chance he may never call again.

Thursday morning Liz woke to the ding of a new text message from Antoinne on her cell phone. "Good Morning". Liz typed back "Same to you, did you sleep well?" Liz laid there for what seemed like hours for his response which actually came exactly one minute later. "I slept great, just left the gym, I have an early meeting can I call you tonight?" Liz replied, "I would like that, have a great day" She climbed out of bed, stripped off her pajamas and on her way to the shower she caught a glimpse of herself naked in the bathroom mirror. "Great he's leaving the gym and I look like walking cellulite! Maybe on our first date I should just wear house shoes and a moo-moo." Yeah this was going to be humiliating she thought. Liz was 5'4" tall and 155 pounds of woman, she certainly wasn't what one would call frail. What if they meet for coffee and he sees her and runs out the door without even a hello? Or worse what if he just flat out tells her he expected she would be prettier? Oh my gosh, would someone really say that? Well, if they would Liz knew she would be the one that it would be said to, that was just how her life went. She wasn't what one would call a negative person. She was actually very upbeat and friendly and full of positive things to say about other people, she just accepted the fact that she wasn't born under a lucky star. If the truth be told she was probably born under a falling star. Regardless of all the new things she had to worry about Liz was excited. She put on a cute sundress and a pair of high strappy sandals for work. Her hair, which was too thick and naturally curly, seemed to actually cooperate this morning. A little plum eyeliner showed off her deep set, dark brown eyes. She tied a pink scarf around her hair and let her locks just fall where they may. She just needed her pink lip gloss and she was ready to go. Liz had a thirty-minute drive to meet with her agent. She was a writer for a travel magazine, it wasn't nearly as glamorous as it sounded but it allowed her to work around Jackson's schedule. She was able to come and go as she needed so she never missed a football game, or even a practice. It was important to her to be there for all of her son's activities. His father had only made it to two games in the past six years. Liz couldn't imagine any place else she would rather be than right there watching her son. On her way to work Liz pulled her SUV into the drive through of Starbucks for her extra hot, nonfat, latte. "Truly the perfect start to any day" she said out loud to no one. This morning she was meeting with her agent to collect her contract for the article on Hilton Head Island, her destination next week. Since Jackson had Friday off school, he would be able to accompany her to South Carolina. It was always nice to be able to take him along on her business trips and it helped her to give the article a family friendly feel for her readers. When he wasn't with her, she generally did her articles more for singles or couples. Sometimes the magazine didn't even send her to the destination she was writing about, instead Liz got her information from online sources, and blogs. She loved traveling and if she had to go more than a few weeks without an escape from the day to day routine of life she became extremely restless. She often wondered if this restlessness of hers was why she never married. Jackson's father had proven to be more of a toad than a frog with potential. She knew she loved him once, but now for the life of her she couldn't understand how or why. It was more of a physical connection than an emotional one. Unfortunately, this was the routine for Liz, she often allowed her body to make decisions her brain would fight. When it came to men, logic was never one of Liz's best qualities. For such a smart woman she made really stupid decisions in the romance department. Liz pulled into her agent's office to collect her contract for her new series of articles on Great Beaches. She was looking forward to visiting ten great beach destinations. This assignment would keep her busy for the next several months and would take her on some amazing trips. The receptionist handed Liz a large gold envelope when she walked in the door. "Hi Liz, Angela had to run out. She said to give this to you, it includes your itineraries for the beaches, I went ahead and booked your villa for you. All of your e-ticket information is inside here."

"Thanks Sweetie, you are amazing. Tell Angela I will be in touch and she can expect my Hilton Head article in two weeks." Liz said as she turned to head back to her car. "Have a great day!" Liz had some extra time to run to the mall and pick up a few things for Jackson before heading to his football practice. He was growing so fast it seemed like Liz had to buy him new clothes or shoes every month. She walked into the mall and headed to for the latest and greatest in teenage apparel. After two stores she had bought three new pair of shorts, four t-shirts, new gym shoes and a new bathing suit. He was set for Hilton Head. Liz wandered through the mall window shopping when she spotted a sexy black dress in a shop window. "Wish I had someplace to wear that!" Liz mumbled under her breath. She decided to go in and just take a look at the dress up close. It was stunning, empire waist, just above the knee, cap sleeve to help hide the arm fat, and a great plunging neckline. Liz immediately thought of Antoinne. She was really excited about the prospect of actually having a date to wear a dress like this one. Her mind started to wander as she imagined what it would be like to feel his hand on the small of her back, leading her around the dance floor. The sales girl interrupted the fantasy, "Would you like a fitting room?"

"Yes, actually I think I would, thank you." The woman took the black dress from Liz. She browsed the store and found two other sundresses for her upcoming trip. She tried on the black dress first. It was perfect, well it would have been better in a size 6, but even in the 10, it wasn't too bad, she thought. The first sundress was a pink and white large floral print, very southern and great for South Carolina. The second dress was a cornflower blue A-line. Liz decided to buy all three. She knew she better leave the mall before she spent any more money. She still had one stop to make at the market to pick up something for dinner. She was trying to lose a few pounds, as always, so a nice salad with some grilled chicken on it would be perfect for tonight's dinner. Walking through the grocery she picked up a bottle of wine and a six pack of beer just in case this date with Antoinne actually happened. It was an upscale market, so she was able to find a nice bottle without too much trouble. Liz allowed her mind to wander. What if this actually turned into something nice? Wouldn't it be nice to have a man around again? She thought. Someone to just have dinner with. Well she had a lot more than dinner on her mind, but it was better not to rush these things. She got in the car and called her sister Caroline. "Hey Care, how are you?"

"Hey Liz, I'm doing alright I am just getting ready to take Emma to her piano lesson." Liz's sister had six kids. Liz wasn't sure how on earth she managed four boys and two girls every single day. She could barely keep up with Jackson's schedule she couldn't imagine how she would do it times six. Caroline was a stay at home mom, so that helped a little but still even the laundry for that many children was overwhelming. "Ok well I won't keep you, I was just wondering if maybe Jackson could come hang out at your place this weekend, I may have a date." Liz hated even mentioning the possibility of a date to her sister she knew there would be a thousand questions to follow but it was better to have to tell her sister than her mother. Her mother would share it with the world and grill her for an hour about what he did and where he was from, and if she thought she should be dating when Jackson was at such an impressionable age. Yes, asking Caroline to babysit was certainly a better way to go. "Sure, he can come over, who are you going out with?" Caroline questioned.

"Well I am not positive yet, but I think I have a date with a new guy his name is Antoinne, he has no kids, owns his own technology company, and has an MBA from MIT".

"So, what's wrong with him?" Caroline asked.

"I am guessing he is a premature ejaculator" Liz replied in a matter of fact tone.

"Well there are worse things, you will get more sleep that way" Caroline mocked.

"Yeah great, can't wait!" Liz replied sounding a bit deflated.

"Ok, well I will call you later I have to get Emma to piano lessons."

"Ok I will call you when I know plans are definite, thanks. Bye"

"Bye"

Liz plugged her phone into her car charger and pulled up to football practice. Jackson was playing the position of wide receiver. Liz didn't know all that much about football, not nearly as much as she should considering the amount of time she spent watching her son practice and going to his games. One thing she did know for sure is that wide receivers took hard hits. She didn't like seeing her son catch the ball and then be knocked to the ground by a stampede of cattle sized boys running toward him full tilt. Unfortunately, football was Jackson's first love so there wasn't much Liz could do except keep the hospital on speed dial and pray a lot. Liz preferred he stay football crazy as opposed to his other obsession which was girls. Football was a safer sport than girls that much she knew to be true. Jackson gave her a quick wave and kept practicing. He always kept an eye out for her, whether it was at practice or at the biggest game of the year she would see him scanning the crowd until he found her. His eyes would meet hers he would flash a quick, crooked smile and then go back to his game. He never said it out loud, but Liz knew her son took a lot of comfort in knowing she was close by. One of the other football moms would always comment on Jackson waving to her and scanning the crowd until he found his mother's face. "My son would never notice if I was here or not." She would say. "It's so sweet how he always needs to know where you are and that you are watching him." It was sweet, and the fact that even other moms noticed gave her a warm feeling about the special bond she shared with her son. He could be a hand full and more days than not his mischievous behavior brought extra stress in to Liz's life which she certainly could have lived without. After practice Liz drove Jackson straight home to hit the showers, thank goodness the weather was still warm enough to keep the windows open, nothing quite compared to the smell of a boy after two hours of football practice. Jackson showered and started on his homework while Liz made dinner. She decided to forego the salads and opt for one of Jackson's favorites. Over their turkey burgers and sweet potato fries he told her how great practice had gone, his excitement and enthusiasm was a quality that Liz loved. She knew it was something most adults lost as time went on, but young people had such a zest for life, Liz admired that feature so much in her son. She cleaned up the kitchen as Jackson finished his homework. By 8:30 he was beginning to fall asleep watching television. She kissed him on the forehead and suggested he turn in early. Most nights during football season were like this. A full day of school, two hours of practice, and then homework took up all his energy. Jackson hugged her and headed off to bed. Liz finally had a quiet moment and began to wonder if she would hear from Antoinne. She had his number in her phone, but she would never call him. Liz knew from years of conversations over several thousand cups of the world's strongest coffee at her grandmother's kitchen table that calling him would pretty much be considered a cardinal sin by any woman over 50. It would be right up there with stealing. She could hear her grandmother's thick old-world accent telling her again and again "Honey you will never find a husband if you show him you care more than he does" she would say. Liz wanted to tell her that finding a husband had been crossed off her "to do" list long ago but she knew it would just make her grandmother worry about her. Grandma thought it best if a woman had a man around to take care of her and look after things. Liz couldn't completely disagree, it would be nice, but she knew she could take care of herself if she had to, and it was looking more and more like that would be the case for her. She changed into her nightgown and washed off her makeup, applied her nightly doses of anti-aging remedies, and after her face was coated in $300.00 worth of miracle products which all guaranteed to make her look twenty-five again, she crawled into bed with a book. Ten minutes later her cell phone rang. Liz smiled when Antoinne's name flashed across her screen.

"Hello" Liz said in a quiet pillow talk voice.

"Hi Sweetie, I didn't wake you, did I?" Antoinne asked.

"Actually no, my husband just left for work, he's on the night shift so your timing is perfect." Liz said.

Antoinne laughed "Please tell me you are kidding."

"Yes, I am kidding" Liz smirked.

"Good, so tell me how your day was?" Antoinne asked with genuine interest. Liz had a gift of gab and there were rarely moments of awkward silence in her life, so she proceeded with ease to tell him all of the events of her day. He seemed to take a real interest in Jackson, asking questions about his football practice that Liz couldn't answer with any real certainty. She did know his primary position, but she couldn't think of the other position he played.

"Well maybe sometime I can check out one of his games with you" Antoinne said. Liz took this as a great sign. Clearly, he wanted to see her, and it sounded like he had a real interest in pursuing something that may resemble a relationship.

"That would be fun, but I should tell you every time he gets knocked down you will have to hold me tight, so I don't jump the fence and run out onto the field" Liz teased.

"Oh, I think I am up for the job" Antoinne played back.

"What about your day handsome, was it good?" Liz really wanted to know more about this man.

"It was really busy I am just driving home now, I had a late meeting downtown. I am exhausted. All day I kept thinking I wish this day would end so I can call Liz and hear her beautiful voice again" Antoinne said flirtatiously.

"That is very sweet" Liz replied using her sexiest voice.

"So, I don't think I can wait much longer to meet you, I was wondering if you wanted to get together tomorrow night?" Antoinne asked.

Liz knew the rules. If he doesn't ask by Wednesday, then he doesn't see you on the weekend. Who was the idiot behind that rule? Liz wondered to herself. She didn't even know this man existed until Wednesday so surely this would be the exception to the outdated rule. "I think that sounds great" Liz answered.

"Terrific, I will pick you up at seven, we will go to dinner and a movie if that's ok with you?" Antoinne had taken complete charge of the plans and it was refreshingly romantic. Liz hated it when men would say "Well I don't care, what do you want to do?" Liz had to make every decision every day, just once it would be nice to have someone else take the reins and just handle it.

"That sounds perfect" She knew her sister Caroline would have an absolute stroke when she found out she was allowing this man she had never met pick her up at her home, but it seemed so unromantic to meet him somewhere. She had a good feeling about Antoinne, so she decided to trust it and just let things take their natural course. Liz and Antoinne continued to talk until midnight. He told her about his childhood, he was the oldest of two children, grew up in Flint, Michigan and like most people from Southeastern Michigan he had a father who worked for the auto industry. He came from the same typical middle-class home she did. Liz was the oldest of three, father also worked for the auto industry, but in Detroit and she grew up about 35 miles south of Flint, in a small town, her father was an engineer, he too worked for auto industry. Liz found herself sharing details about her life that she had never really shared with any man. She told him about being the product of teenage parents and feeling more like the parent than the child in her relationship with her mother. She told him how she had always felt that it if it weren't for the village of grandparents and extended family, she doesn't know what would have happened to her and her sister. Liz's brother was much younger, and he had a very different childhood than Liz and Caroline had. Theirs had been one where they were loved but a lot of their needs and wants were simply neglected because their parents were still kids and trying to navigate their way through what was difficult for people to do in thirties, let alone in their early twenties. Liz and Antoinne both enjoyed a taste for some of life's finer things and loved to travel. Both were avid basketball fans. Growing up Antoinne had been a big athlete, Liz wasn't really into sports as a kid, she had always been too self-conscious of her weight to try and even attempt anything athletic. Both of their parents were still married to each other. Both had strict fathers, and mothers who stayed home to take care of their children. He did not share the same closeness with his family now as Liz did with hers, but she assumed a part of that was physical distance. Antoinne's father had recently retired and his parents moved from their home in Flint, Michigan to Macon, Georgia. His mother had grown up in Georgia and had always wanted to go back home. He saw them every few months. His sister attended college in Tennessee, she was several years younger than he was and although they spoke on the phone weekly, he didn't see her very often. Liz saw her parents and siblings every few days. She had a large extended family and she knew it was somewhat overwhelming for newcomers, so she didn't talk too much about it until she was sure they weren't going to run. Finally, at midnight they said, "Good night." Liz hung up the phone and started to dial Jenna, but she realized it was too late and disconnected before it rang. Liz really wanted to tell someone about this amazing man. If he looked half as good as he sounded, she was in huge trouble.

Chapter 2

Antoinne Fredericks was a strong, quiet disciplined man, he strived for success in everything every aspect of his life. Growing up in Flint, Michigan he saw the harder parts of life one sees in the inner city. He had watched childhood friends go down the wrong path and end up in jail or dead. He was not going to allow that to be his legacy. He came from a hardworking, middle class, church going family. His dad like many black men from his generation was a strict disciplinarian who showed little affection and offered less praise. They did not have a close relationship, there was love there but it never developed into friendship. They shared a strong pride and a stubbornness that prevented them both from overcoming the obstacles and walls between a father with high expectations and a son who felt like he could never quite meet those demands. His parents' marriage was one of convenience and habit more than lifelong friendship, they fought a lot and often spent time apart, having homes in two states made it easy to take frequent breaks without ever really having to address their marital issues.

Antoinne was a good son in spite of their lack of closeness. He took his grandmother and mother to church every Sunday. He checked on them and called regularly and was always there to lend a helping hand. Antoinne left Flint when he went off to college at eighteen. He received scholarships and financial aid and was determined he would not work on the line in the auto industry like most of the men in his family had done for their entire lives. He knew it was good job and he should have probably been more grateful at the offers to help get him in the union, but he had bigger dreams. He wanted to be his own boss, he wasn't good at taking orders from anyone and the thought of punching a clock for forty years made his throat feel like it was closing. Antoinne's father was a bit jealous of his son. He saw him as arrogant and even though he was proud of him he could not really relate to him. Antoinne received his bachelor's degree in Information Technology from Oakland University and went on to receive his MBA from MIT before the age of twenty-four. After college he spent a year working in California for a startup in Silicon Valley before the masses of people and traffic drove him back to his midwestern roots. When returning to Southeast Michigan Antoinne and his college roommate started their own company. They provided internet set up and security to the four large sports franchises in Detroit. They had another friend from college who helped them land the gig and their little company soared to success overnight. He worked hard to keep it going. He often was up half the night on his computer and slept very little the first few years. By twenty-seven he had a full team in place, and he expanded his interests to include real estate, he bought houses to flip and sell and owned six rental properties on the northwest side of Detroit. He and his college girlfriend had made a few attempts to work out their on again off again relationship but they seemed to fight too much and he knew it was time to move on and find someone who shared his goals and interests, he needed a woman in his life who was not so self-absorbed and always flirting with other men to make him jealous, he was getting too old to keep playing these kinds of games.

Friday morning Liz cleaned her house from top to bottom before deciding to treat herself to a manicure and pedicure. She generally always had a clean house, although living with a twelve-year-old certainly made it a daunting task. The floors were washed, everything was dusted, and as usual she spent most of her time cleaning in Jackson's room. Sometimes she wondered how on earth she could have such a sloppy child. Liz wished he would have inherited her need for cleanliness. She knew it bordered obsessive compulsive behavior, but she couldn't stand it if anything was out of place. Finally, with that done she headed to the nail salon. As Liz pulled into the parking lot her phone rang, it was Antoinne. "Hello" she said sweetly.

"Hi Beautiful, how is your day going?" He asked.

"Wonderful, I am just going in to get a manicure, how about you?" She replied.

"It's good, I am on my way to a meeting and when I finish up, I am going to go home to get showered and changed for our date tonight." Liz smiled he sounded just as excited as she was feeling.

"Well good, I am really looking forward to seeing you" Liz said.

"Is the Real Seafood Company, downtown alright for dinner? I wasn't sure if you liked seafood or not." Antoinne asked.

"I love it, and it sounds wonderful" Liz replied.

"Ok great, well Sweetie go enjoy your manicure and I will see you at seven. OH, and could you text me your address before you go in, so I know where I am going tonight?"

"Oh gosh! I guess that would help wouldn't it?" Liz laughed. "I will send it right now, and I will see you at seven"

"Sounds good" Antoinne replied. "Bye" Liz hung up the phone and quickly typed her address into a text message and hit send.

She wanted to feel pretty for her date, so she decided on a simple French manicure, classic but elegant she thought. Liz had chosen to wear the new cornflower blue A-line dress. It was sweet but still sexy. It showed just the right amount of cleavage. She paired the dress with a light yellow short sleeved, cropped cardigan sweater and an open toed sandal that wasn't too high, she certainly did not want to fall on her face. The dress came almost to her knee, she had nice legs, so Liz felt pretty good when she put it on. She felt very lucky they were enjoying a beautiful Indian summer in Michigan, it was early September, but it was still warm enough for her to wear sandals and a summer dress this evening. In a few short weeks she would packing those things away for fall sweaters and blue jeans and bracing for the long Michigan winter. She loved the first snowfall but once Christmas was over Liz was ready for Spring.   Her fingers and toes looked great with their new French tips. Her sister Caroline was picking Jackson up from practice and taking him back to her house for the night, so Liz went home to shower and get ready for her date. Her biggest challenge was always the hair. She decided to straighten it and flip the ends up, her hair was long and thick it was a light brown with blond highlights. It would take her a good hour to get it straightened and shiny and flipped just enough to make it look like it took no effort. It was a bit of a younger look and since Antoinne was five years her junior she figured it was best to work every angle to her advantage. She lined her eyes in a soft smoky grey and put a high gloss on her lips. She applied a touch of perfume behind her ears and her knee, slipped into her dress, put on a silver bracelet and silver hoop earrings, and she was ready with 15 minutes to spare. She really wanted to have a glass of wine to calm her nerves before he arrived, but she thought it may look bad to be drinking alone when he arrived. She certainly didn't want to give the impression she drank a lot. So instead she fussed with her hair and touched up her gloss. The doorbell rang. She gave herself one more glance in the mirror and decided it was too late to make any changes and headed for the door.

Liz's heart was pounding out of her chest as she reached for the knob. She opened it to see Antoinne standing before her in a beautiful bronze colored cashmere sweater and dark jeans. He looked far better in person than his profile picture on the site. This man was gorgeous. He stood about six foot tall. His head was shaved bald. He had piercing brown eyes and skin the color of rich, dark chocolate. His sweater was fitted, and she could see the definition of muscles in his chest. He did not have an ounce of fat on his body she thought to herself. "Hi, come in" Liz said nervously.

"You look great" he smiled as he gave her body a once over from head to toe. "Do I get a hug?" he asked.

"Of course," Liz replied. She stepped closer, put her arms around his neck and let her body slide against him. He smelled wonderful. There were instant sparks between them.

Liz backed up before she did something stupid like kiss him. She felt the heat rising from her toes just being close to him. "Please come in" Liz said, walking from the entry toward the living room.

"You have a nice place here" Antoinne remarked as he looked around. "Do I get the tour?"

"Sure" Liz said. Antoinne slipped his hand in hers as she began to walk him through the house. It wasn't a big home so it wouldn't take long. It was an open floor plan so from the living room the kitchen was clearly visible. She took him toward the hall where Jackson's room, the main bathroom and the spare room were located. Thank goodness she had cleaned Jackson's room Liz thought to herself. She then turned and walked back through the living room and toward the other side of the house where the master bedroom was located. The floor plan was an open ranch, so everything was very easy to see from the main part of the house. Still hand in hand they entered her bedroom, she pointed out the bathroom and the small sitting room area she used as an office. As Liz turned to lead them back to the living room Antoinne gave her hand a slight tug, pulling her close into him. He pulled her mouth to his. His full lips were soft and gentle. "I've been thinking about kissing you all day" he whispered. Liz knew she was in huge trouble. She pulled away.

"Would you like a beer or a glass of wine?" She asked.

"Sure, I would love a beer" Antoinne replied as he made himself comfortable on the brown leather loveseat.

"Glass or bottle?" Liz asked.

"Bottle is fine" He responded. Liz decided she would pour herself a glass of white wine. She carried the drinks into the living room and sat next to Antoinne on the loveseat.

"Thank you" he said taking the bottle from her hand.

"Your house is nice, you work and raise a child on your own and still manage to keep your house spotless, I'm impressed" She liked that he noticed. Liz couldn't stand a lot of clutter and was glad to hear someone appreciate her need for organization and cleanliness.

"It's not spotless, but I try" she smiled and slid in next to him. Antoinne put his hand on her leg.

"You look really pretty tonight, they did a nice job on your nails." He said taking her hand in his and kissing the top of it.

"Well thank you sir" she smiled shyly. They made small talk while they finished their drinks. Liz only lived about three blocks from the restaurant and it was an unusually warm night, so they decided to walk to dinner. The Real Seafood Company was located on Main Street in the heart of downtown Ann Arbor. It was surrounded by other restaurants, bars and small businesses. She loved living in a college town. With the University of Michigan campus only a mile from her house she was able to fully submerge herself into the diverse culture that one found near universities.

Liz grabbed a light jacket, he took it from her and held it while she slipped it on. They walked hand in hand, it was a perfect night. There was a nice breeze blowing and the city was alive with people enjoying this last burst of summer before the long winter arrived. For dinner they both ordered fish. She had the red snapper and Antoinne ordered the grilled sea bass. They shared a bottle of wine. Liz was glad to see the food arrive, as she was really beginning to feel the effects of the alcohol. She fed Antoinne a bite of her snapper. His mouth was so sexy she wanted to kiss him again. Conversation flowed with ease. They laughed and talked like they had known each other forever. Antoinne described the house he was going to build in great detail. I am hoping to break ground in the next few weeks, if that doesn't happen then it will be next Spring before we get started because the ground will be frozen in two months. I am still waiting on the permit approvals"

"Did you bring your blueprints with you?" She asked.

"As a matter of fact, I have a set in the trunk of my car, I can show them to you when we get back to house if you like." he replied.

After dinner they walked outside. Liz was happy for the cool breeze she knew the air and the walk would clear the wine fog in her head. As they and headed toward Liz's house they came to a small Blues club where live music was billowing into the street. "Would you like to go in?" He asked.

"Sure, that would be nice" She responded with a smile. They went into the bar and found a small table near the back, it was an old building with hardwood floors and a high ceiling exposing all the duct work that was painted black. The bar was long, it was a dark, masculine hardwood that was probably original to the structure. Liz guessed it was at least fifty years old. The walls were lined with tall back booths and tables that matched the bar and in front of the dance floor there were another cluster of small tables. The music was wonderful, and the place wasn't too crowded yet. Most of the local bars and clubs didn't start to fill up until about eleven. The band had a female singer who had a sultry, soulful voice. She was singing a Mary J Blige song. "Would you like to dance?" Antoinne asked Liz.

"I would love to" she replied. He put his hand on the small of her back and lead her to the dance floor. Liz draped her arms around his neck, Antoinne took her hips in his hands as he led their bodies in to a slow rhythmic glide. He leaned into her, "You smell really good" he whispered in her ear.

"Thank you very much, I was going to say the same thing to you" Liz appreciated it when a man took the time to put on cologne. Antoinne's scent was clean and fresh with a hint of sandalwood. It was making her a little crazy. She wanted to nuzzle into his neck and stay there. Liz knew she shouldn't do it, but she couldn't help herself, she leaned into him and started singing along with the band in his ear. "Time on my hands, since you been away boy, I ain't got no plans, no, no, no, no, and the sound of the rain on my window pain is slowly driving me insane" He smiled and slid his hand further down her back and pulled her body tight against his. She put a small gentle kiss on his neck.

"You are gonna get yourself in trouble" he smiled.

"I guess I should stop then" Liz smirked.

He kissed her softly. Taking her bottom lip between his. "Oh, wow this is dangerous" Antoinne said in a raspy voice.

Their bodies melted together as they continued to dance for three more songs. "How about we get out of here?" he asked.

"I agree, the smoke is really starting to bother me, I could use some fresh air" Liz lied. She knew if she didn't get some space between them soon this night was going to go a lot further than she had planned.

Antoinne helped Liz put her coat back on, paid for their drinks and they walked back out in the cool night air. "That was really nice, and you can sing!" He exclaimed.

"You have had too much to drink!" Liz laughed, knowing that her singing was less than impressive. Antoinne laughed and put his arm around her as they walked back toward Liz's house.

"I really like you Liz" Antoinne said.

"Thank you, I have really enjoyed spending time with you tonight."

As they approached her driveway, he asked "Would you still like to see the house plans?"

"Absolutely, we have definitely missed the movie, but I have an apple pie and I could make a pot of coffee, what do you think?" She asked.

"Well I am not a coffee drinker, but apple pie and a glass of milk would be great" He said as he approached his silver BMW parked in her driveway. "Let me just grab my house plans" he said.

Liz noticed his car was immaculate. "Two points" she thought to herself.
She unlocked the door, hung up her coat and the two headed to the kitchen. While Liz made coffee for herself and sliced the apple pie Antoinne unrolled his blueprints on the table. She poured him a big glass of milk and warmed his pie for 20 seconds in the microwave before adding a scoop of vanilla ice cream to the top. "How did you know apple pie is my favorite?" he asked. Liz knew there wasn't a man in Michigan who did not love apple pie, his mother and grandma would of course been able to make a perfect apple pie, as did Liz's, it was just one of those things that went with living where they lived. Mashed potatoes and apple pie, a staple in every Michigan home.

"Lucky guess" Liz smiled as she set his desert in front of him. She poured her coffee and leaned over the table next to him to look at the house plans. She would never indulge in the apple pie as the dinner and drinks had exceeded her caloric allotment for a week. She was impressed with his attention to detail. He walked her through the prints room by room telling her exactly what he envisioned. She was so attracted to his enthusiasm. It was going to be a beautiful home. He was planning on building it just south of Flint in a rural area about 45 minutes north of Liz.

"I would love to see the property sometime"

"Well maybe we can drive up tomorrow after I take you to breakfast" Antoinne answered. Liz couldn't help but laugh out loud.

"You are smooth" she said shaking her head. Antoinne turned and put his hands on her hips and lifted Liz up and set her on the table in front of him. "Oh my" she whispered. He stood between her legs and leaned in to kiss her. It was perhaps one of the greatest kisses of her life. It was gentle but urgent. He slid his tongue into her mouth sending sparks through her body. She reached up and stroked his bald head. Antoinne moaned softly. His hands rubbed her thighs. He gripped her neck and pulled her mouth tight against his. His mouth became more forceful in its desire. "I want you, I want you so much" he whispered. This man was causing Liz to feel things she hadn't felt in a very long time. She knew she needed to stop, she needed to send him home, but she couldn't. She wanted Antoinne. He pulled back and looked her in the eyes. His hands gently stroked her face. "I want to make love to you. I know we just met, but I feel like I've known you forever. I don't want to be disrespectful in any way. I really like you, so if you want to me leave then tell me now and I will go."

"I want you to stay." Liz whispered. Antoinne took her hands and helped her lower herself off the table. Then, from behind with his hands on her hips he led them to her bedroom. He slid the straps of her dress off her shoulders and let it fall to the floor. She stood before him in her blue panties and matching bra. Antoinne tried to conceal a crooked smile on his face. "Now is really not the time to laugh!" Liz looked at him with shock on her face.

"No, no baby, I think it's really cute to see that your panties and bra are the exact same color as your dress." He kissed her before she could respond. Her fingers moved to the bottom of his sweater and she lifted it over his head, leaving him standing before her in his under shirt and jeans. With urgency she pulled the undershirt from his jeans and ripped it over his head, exposing his bare chest. His skin was smooth and soft. His muscles bulged under her touch. He was physical perfection. Her hands moved to his back pulling him tight against her. She kissed his neck. Her mouth sucking gently on his skin. He unhooked her bra and tossed it the floor. He cupped her large breasts in his hands and welcomed them into his mouth.

Antoinne backed Liz up to the bed and laid her down with his body on top of hers. His legs parted hers. His mouth enveloped hers with urgency while his hands caressed her breasts. Liz reached for him, undoing his belt and the button of his pants. Her hands could feel his hardness through his jeans. She let out a soft moan. "Wow what have you been hiding there?" she whispered. He laughed and kissed her softly. His fingers moved to her panties lowering them from her hips, leaving her exposed and naked for his approval. She watched with wanting eyes as he stood up and took off his pants. His body was hard and defined. He was dark and muscular with a powerful erection. He was physically perfect. Antoinne took his time, gently navigating the curves of her hips with his soft kisses, his hands stroking her hair, he was memorizing every inch of her and exploring her with loving admiration. Liz wanted to devour him, she had not wanted any man this much as long as she could remember. She couldn't get enough of him, she wanted this man inside of her. Liz gasped as Antoinne lowered his body on to hers filling her with waves of ecstasy. Their bodies moved together in perfect rhythm. He looked into her eyes and kissed her softly, stroking her face. "You are so beautiful" he whispered. Liz knew she was already falling in love with him.

Chapter 3

Liz awoke to Antoinne kissing her shoulder. His naked body wrapped perfectly around hers. "Good morning Baby" he whispered in her ear. "Oh wow" Liz thought to herself. She couldn't believe he woke up before she did. She would have preferred to have brushed her teeth and showered before he opened his eyes.
"Good morning" she said with her back still toward him. She rolled gently away and put her legs on the floor, willing them not to collapse under her when she stood, it had been a long time since a man had made love to her like that, and today she was bound to feel a few reminders. She walked to the master bathroom with his eyes glued to her naked body. She was wondering if he was shocked by what he saw in the light of day. She shut the door and turned on the water so he wouldn't hear her pee. She knew she was being ridiculous but there is always that first morning awkwardness when you wake up next to someone for the first time. Liz brushed her teeth and started the shower. She felt like perhaps she was being a little rude, but she still had last night's makeup running down her eyes and she really didn't want to greet Antoinne looking that way. She stepped into the steaming hot shower, tilting her head up under the water and letting it cascade over her. She heard him step into the bathroom. Her eyes opened quickly but she immediately shut them again, pretending not to notice his presence. She was surprised to hear him pee but it's kind of relaxed her a little. "Ok Liz, this is fine, just relax" she thought to herself. "There is a package of new toothbrushes in the bottom drawer on the right, help yourself, I insist!" she yelled out from under the stream of hot water.
"Funny, real funny" he responded laughingly. She heard the drawer open and then the familiar sound of brushing began. He seemed to brush for a long time, she wondered if he always did that or if it was for her benefit. She squeezed shampoo into her hand and began to lather her hair when he stepped into the shower to join her.
"I'll do that for you" he said putting his hands into the lather and rubbing her scalp. Liz turned to allow him to get the back for her as well, it felt wonderful. He squeezed the liquid soap onto her bath puff and began washing her shoulders and arms. His hands moved down her backside as he lathered her body. He turned her to face him and did the same to the front of her. He didn't take his eyes off of her. He gently massaged the puff over her breasts, lifting

her arms and washing every inch of her skin. He knelt in front of her while water poured over them washing each foot and working his way up her legs. She had never had a man completely wash her body before. He licked the water running off of her stomach. Sliding his hand between her legs he stroked her body, gently massaging between her legs, bringing her to orgasm with his fingers. Liz had to hold tight to his shoulders to keep from falling. With one swift move Antoinne pulled her down onto him. He penetrated her so quickly she gasped. Water cascaded over them as she her hips moved up and down on his body, taking him deeper into her with every thrust. He kissed her forcefully, his warm, wet tongue exploring her mouth. Faster and harder they moved in unison as his body was overtaken by animal urgency. Liz's arms were wrapped tight around Antoinne's neck, she needed to be as close to him as she could possibly be. He circled his fingers in her long, wet hair and pulled her head back, his mouth hungrily taking her neck, his tongue tracing circles on her clavicle bones. No part of her body escaped his touch. He wanted to know every inch of her, claim her as his own. "Does that feel good?" He whispered.

"Oh yes" she moaned softly. "God yes" Again she felt her self-climaxing, she fell into him and let him take command of their journey. His strong hands gripped her hips guiding them up and down for his own pleasure, he watched the steaming water pour over her milky white skin turning it hot and pink. He couldn't stop. Faster and harder their bodies moved as one. "Oh Baby" he moaned. "Take it, take it all" he whispered.

"Oh God" She murmured as she felt his warm heat explode inside of her. They stayed intertwined together for several minutes until the water began to cool. Liz stood and took Antoinne's hand pulling him to his feet. She quickly lathered the shower puff and began to rewash her body, as the temperature of the water started to plummet. Antoinne poured the soap into his hands and lathered himself as fast as he could. The shower turned icy. They were laughing as they took turns dashing in and out of the water to rinse off. Once the soap was finally gone, she turned off the faucet and reached for towels for them. "Shower sex always seems like a good idea, but you forget how quickly the hot water runs out!" Liz said shaking from the cold.

"It was worth it" Antoinne said as he leaned over and gave her a quick kiss.

Liz dressed in pair of blue jeans and a pink, chenille pullover. "Your clothes smell like smoke from the club last night, do you want me to toss them in the wash?"

"No sweetie, I have a bag for the gym in my car, it has everything I need, fresh clothes, contact solution and deodorant". Liz took his keys and walked out to her driveway to get his bag for him. While he dressed in jogging pants a t-shirt and hooded sweatshirt, she did her hair and makeup. No time for straightening today, it would have to be the all-natural, curly look.

"I like your hair curly, it's sexy" Antoinne commented when Liz came out of the bathroom. "Now let's go get something to eat, I am starving!"

Liz smiled, "Me too." Antoinne opened the passenger door to his BMW for her. "Where to?" He asked backing the car up.

"There is a great place about fifteen minutes north of the city, if you feel like taking me to see your property we can stop there on the way. They make fantastic French toast."

"That sounds good, I would really like you to see it." He leaned over and kissed her quickly. Antoinne held her hand while he drove. They arrived at the small family restaurant, he opened her door and they went in to enjoy the world's best French toast. Liz had several cups of coffee, Antoinne stuck with orange juice. They chatted over breakfast about the property, and Jackson. He said he was looking forward to being able to meet her son, but Liz wasn't quite sure she was ready for that just yet. Logically she should take her time and make sure he was going to be around for a while before allowing Jackson to meet him, she knew things were moving way too fast, but she couldn't stop it. Since Jackson's dad really wasn't a regular part of his life Liz knew her son ached for a father figure and would grow attached to Antoinne very quickly. Probably just as quickly as Liz was. She told him of her upcoming trip to Hilton Head, and her contract to write articles on ten amazing beaches. "I want to see a few of those beaches with you." Antoinne said, as he leaned forward and pushed her hair out of her eyes.

"I would like that." Liz smiled. She stared into his deep brown eyes, feeling butterflies in her stomach. It hit her in a flash as she thought "I've known him for less than twenty-four hours and already I would miss him if he were gone." That thought terrified her to her very core. "How was this happening so fast? How did she feel this way already?" Liz wondered. "Should we go?" He asked.

"Sure, I'm ready." Antoinne left a twenty on the table for their breakfast. She stood and slipped her hand in his as they walked back to his car. It was about another twenty-five-minute drive before they arrived at his property. As he drove, he kept his hand on her leg and told her about the problems he had been having with getting his building permits. He had found out after buying the property that there was a rare, protected bird who made its home there. His lawyer was trying to work out the details, but it was certainly causing him some added stress. "If they tell me I can't build on it, the property is useless." He told her as they pulled off the road and onto a dirt drive. He stopped the car. "We will need to walk the rest from here." He had cleared a narrow path through the center of the land for walking. It was thick with brush and trees. The area he was planning to put the house was on a bit of a hill. It was a peaceful, wonderful place. Liz liked it and had a quick flash of her and Antoinne and Jackson sitting in front of the fireplace playing a game. "What do think?" Antoinne asked.

"I think it's beautiful and private and I love it." She said enthusiastically. He pulled her close to him and hugged her hard. She wrapped her arms around his waist and put her ear to his heart, she could have stayed there in the safety of his arms forever. Liz knew right at that moment that no matter how crazy or illogical it was, she was falling in love with him. He took her hand and they walked back to the car. He opened her door for her, Liz closed her eyes and leaned her head back. Antoinne started the car and backed out onto the road. "You look sleepy Beautiful" He commented.

"Well I don't think we slept more than about four hours last night." She teased, poking him gently in his stomach. "I really should go get Jackson, my sister is probably getting ready to send out a search party." Liz was beginning to miss her son, but she was torn she certainly didn't want to leave Antoinne.

"Yeah I know you do, I need to get some work done today too." Antoinne said with a sigh. He turned the car south and headed back toward her house. He pulled into the driveway and put the car in park but didn't turn off the engine. "Ok sweetie you go gets your boy. I need to go to check on a couple of my rental properties." He leaned over taking her face in his hands and began to kiss her softly. "Wow, I don't want to leave." he whispered.

"I feel the same way, I would much rather go inside and curl up in your arms and take a nap. I wish I could." Liz said.

"Can I see you before you leave for Hilton Head?" He asked.

"Yeah I don't leave until Thursday." She replied, stroking the top of his hand.

"Ok, I will call you later, be careful driving to your sister's Baby." He said. Antoinne gave her one more kiss before Liz opened the door and stepped out of the car. She hit the code to enter her garage, so she could get straight into her SUV to go pick up Jackson. Liz started her truck and called her sister to tell her she was on her way. She then immediately dialed Jenna while she drove the thirty-five minutes to her sister's so she could tell her about the amazing night she just had.

"Hey Pal, how was your date?" Jenna asked.

"It just ended five minutes ago." Liz responded.

"So, I take it that it went well then?" Jenna said laughingly. Liz told Jenna every amazing detail of her night, and morning with Antoinne. "So, do you think he will call you later or was it a hit and run?" Jenna teased.

"Bitch please! I've got that man hooked! It's a wrap, he's mine." Liz said jokingly. "No seriously I think he will call, we really had a great time together. I know I shouldn't have slept with him on the first date, but I couldn't help it, everything just clicked. It was like I had known him for at least a week." She exclaimed, as they both burst into laughter. "I'm pretty sure he is going to call; the trick will be to wait and not call him first."

"I'm sure you will hear from him by tonight, but if you don't then you just have to stay calm. Whatever you do, don't call him and don't text him. Let him come to you." Jenna lectured.

"Yeah, yeah." Liz replied in an exasperated tone, suddenly the lesbian was an expert on male, female relationships she thought. Liz knew Jenna was right. She couldn't do anything at this point except wait. She had to wait to see how he reacted once he was away from her. Would he be just as crazy about her as she was about him? Hopefully it wasn't going to be one of those "out of sight, out of mind" things, Liz worried. She knew they really connected, so she was pretty sure he would call but there was still that annoying voice in the back of her head creating doubt. That voice that said "Well slut you ruined it, men only want women they have to chase, and you gave away the milk for free your big cow so it's over before it really even gets started. Way to go." Liz had to wonder why the voice sounded so much like her sisters. She pulled into get her son, and tried to put on her best "No I didn't sleep with him" face and walked in. Jackson was close by and Liz was relieved her sister wouldn't be able to ask her much about the date until later, she knew the guilty pleasure would be all over her face.

"Hi, did you have fun?" Caroline asked.

"Yeah, we had a great time, he's really nice." Liz replied as casually as she could.

"Great. What did you do?" she questioned.

"We walked to The Real Seafood Company for dinner and then went to that Jazz club on Liberty. It was a lot of fun." Liz replied.

"Good, do you want some coffee?" Caroline asked.

"No thanks, I think we are just going to head home, I have to get some preliminary work done for my article on Hilton Head and I am pretty tired. Thanks for keeping Jackson for me." She answered.

"Yeah, thanks for having my Aunt Care" Jackson added.

"Anytime, Sweets" she said hugging him. "You have a great time in Hilton Head."

"It would be better if I could take a friend." Jackson replied, giving his mom a pleading look.

"Come on you, let's go." Liz said ignoring his request. Jackson picked up his bag, Liz put a hand on his shoulder, and they turned to leave. "Bye Care, thanks again" Liz said on her way out.

"Anytime, call me later" she responded.

When Liz and Jackson returned home, Jackson went to the neighbors to play basketball. Liz pulled the sheets off her bed, she stopped to hold the pillow to her face, the smell of Antoinne's cologne filled her senses bringing flashes of their night so fast and furiously to the forefront of her memory chills ran down her spine. "What if he doesn't call?" she wondered aloud. She immediately dismissed that thought, Liz has been with enough men to know that magic like that is rare and she is sure he knows it too. She unconsciously begins to hum the song she sang for him on the dance floor as she walked the sheets to the washer. Liz added her favorite lavender fabric softener and decided she should get some research done for her upcoming trip to Hilton Head. She needed to make sure they hit the local hot spots and tourist attractions. Liz likes to also include a few hidden treasures when she writes her articles, so her readers don't get the same information every time they look into a vacation spot. She wants to offer something for everyone and include the nearby attractions. Everyone knows Hilton Head is the place for golfers, so she will touch on it, but her focus would be on the great beaches and out of the way shops and restaurants. She headed to her small office off her bedroom. Instead of sitting down in front of her computer she sat back on the chaise lounge chair and pulled her favorite blanket over her. She decided on a short nap before getting to work. In a matter of seconds her eyes were closed, and she was sound asleep. Liz awoke an hour later to the tweet of a new text message on her cell phone. It was from Antoinne. "Hi beautiful, I can't quit thinking about you" Liz cast her pretend fishing pole into the air and began to reel it in. "Gotcha" she whispered. She knew it was bad luck to be so confident, but she was elated this man was feeling the same way she was. She texts him back. "I had to take a nap, you wore me out!" She knew the male ego well enough to know he would enjoy hearing that he left her spent.

He text back again "Good I plan on doing it again soon! I will call you as soon as finish up with this project I am working on. xoxoxo" Liz was thrilled. She had an instant spring in her step. She went to the kitchen and made a pot of coffee before settling in on her Hilton Head research. She made notes on little restaurants for her and Jackson to check out. They would be staying in a beach house in the Sea Pines district, it was her favorite location on the island. Jackson would love being able to ride a bicycle all over the resort community. The beach was typical of South Carolina, it had tall grasses and large trees dripping with Spanish moss. It is truly the epitome of old southern charm. There was nothing better to a Michigan girl than to sit on the shore of the Atlantic Ocean, or any ocean and watch the sunset. She wondered if the people who lived there saw it the same way she did. Did they truly remember to appreciate the daily beauty or were they so accustomed to it that it just became the background one often overlooks? Although people from the south may have thought the same thing about a big snow storm, covering the world in a fresh white blanket of beauty. She knew it was stunning, but she didn't look at it with the same eyes as someone who had never experienced the winter would see it. Liz was anxious to get there. She loved traveling, even the packing was fun to her. She couldn't imagine having a job where she had to sit behind a desk for eight hours a day doing the same thing over and over. Traveling was her passion. She would die of boredom if she had to do anything else. Jackson returned home from the neighbor's house. "I'm starving, are you cooking?" he bellowed through the house. "Shoot kids always want to eat!" She said to herself. "Just order a pizza, I need to finish up a few things for our trip, and I am not in the mood to cook, ok?" she yelled back across the house. That was one of the benefits of not having a man around the house. Twelve-year-old boys were perfectly happy to eat pizza, he didn't care if she cooked or not. "Sure, sounds good. I am going to order it now, what do you want on it?" She wondered why he kept yelling and didn't just walk the 30 feet to her office. "It doesn't matter honey, I'm not hungry. Get whatever you want." Liz could have gotten up and gone to him too, but the yelling seemed to be working so well what was the point? Jackson was a great kid, was a twelve-year-old boy, and common sense wasn't something he had developed as of yet, but he was sweet and funny, and truly the greatest gift she could ever receive. He was already taller than Liz by a few inches. His dad was 6'3" so Liz was pretty sure he was going to keep growing for a while. His big brown eyes and a perfect smile melted the hearts of everyone. His skin was a beautiful shade of caramel. As a baby, people would stop her everywhere she went to tell her what a beautiful baby he was. His soft curls and long lashes made him almost too pretty to be a boy. He had a very outgoing personality and loved to be the star of the show. He was the love of Liz's life. She was extremely overprotective of him. Jackson was a precocious kid and often found himself talking too much in class or fooling around in the halls. Boys being boys as far as Liz was concerned and every teacher and administrator at his middle school knew she was a mama bear and they better be extremely careful when coming after her boy. She knew she needed to work harder at letting him suffer the consequences of his choices but something in her snapped when it came to her baby boy and consequently, he was a bit spoiled and a little too entitled. She was working on it, and so were his coaches. The good thing was he was honest when he did something wrong, he always admitted guilt and tried hard to make it up to the adults he disappointed so he was well liked even though he could be a real handful.

The pizza arrived thirty minutes later. They spread out a blanket on the living room floor and put a movie in the DVD player. Invincible would be their Saturday night feature film, for at least the twentieth time. She didn't mind, as long as she was enjoying it with her baby boy, they could watch it another five hundred times together. Half way through the movie her cell phone rang, Antoinne flashed across her screen. "Keep watching Buddy, I will be back in a few" she said getting up and heading to her room to talk to him privately. "Well hi there" Liz said in a seductive tone.

"Damn woman, what did you do to me? I can't quit thinking about you! I haven't been able to focus on anything today!" Antoinne scolded.

Liz laughed. "Yeah I forgot to warn you, I got it like that." They both laughed.

"So when can I see you again?" He asked.

"Would you like to come over and have dinner with us tomorrow?" She asked, feeling a little nervous about exposing Jackson to him so soon.

"I would love to; do you think your son will be ok with it?"

"Well since he doesn't pay the mortgage, he doesn't get to decide who I entertain, but honestly I think he will adore you." She replied.

They talked for another thirty minutes about what each of them had done that day. Their bond was growing quickly. Finally, Liz told him she needed to get back to the movie she was watching with Jackson.

"So tomorrow at five sound good?" She asked.

"I'll be there. I will call you in the morning. Sweet dreams Baby." Antoinne whispered into the phone.

Chapter 4

Sunday morning Liz pulled out their suitcases and began to pack for the upcoming trip to Hilton Head Island. She was looking forward to spending some time on the beach. She also loved having a few days alone with Jackson. This new puberty thing was unchartered waters for them and has led to some mood swings and behaviors she hadn't quite been able to adjust to just yet. Liz hoped the one on one time with her son will help them reconnect. Lately it seems like there has been more yelling than talking going on between them and she knows the trip will do them both a bit of good. Since Liz travels so often she has become the expert packer, in less than thirty minutes she had them both packed and the suitcases loaded into her walk-in closet, ready to be put in the back of her SUV. She wondered if this would be the last evening, she would get to see Antoinne before she left. How was she getting so attached to him already? Liz knew from past experience that she fell in love quickly and once it hit, it would take an act of God for her to remove this man from her life and her heart. Liz loved very deeply. She was honest and loyal to a fault, and it had taken many relationships for her to realize that not everyone was the same way when it came to love. It had been a painful lesson she had learned more than once. Antoinne seemed different. He was open with her and seemed like he genuinely wanted to get to know her. He said he wasn't really looking for a relationship but if he found one, he would certainly be happy to have it. She felt the same way. Life was full and complete without a man in it, but the nights could be a little lonely, if she met a great guy, she was certainly willing to put her heart out there and take a chance once more. She ran the vacuum and tidied up the house before heading to the grocery store to pick up something for dinner. She was a terrible grocery shopper, wandering up and down the isles aimlessly buying one hundred dollars' worth of beverages and eight dollars' worth of food. She meandered along until she finally decided she would make lasagna for Antoinne. It was something she could have ready ahead of time and not to stand in the kitchen preparing while he was there. She picked up the ingredients she needed, along with things for a fresh salad, and loaf of French bread. For dessert she already knew apple pie was his favorite so she would stop at the local pie shop before heading home to get started on the lasagna. When Liz returned to the house Jackson was finally awake enjoying a bowl of cereal in front of the television where he had been told no more than a million times food was off limits. Liz could feel the irritation rising in her chest. "Did the kitchen burn down while I was gone? Is that why you are eating in the living room?" She asked.

"Sorry" Jackson responded as he picked up his bowl and headed back to the dining room table. Liz knew no matter how many times she said eating in the living room was off limits Jackson would do it every time she left the house, or even the room. It was one battle she just wasn't ready to give up yet although she was losing it on a regular basis.

"Hey, I invited a new friend of mine to dinner tonight" Liz mentioned casually as she unpacked the groceries.

"Is it the guy you went out with Friday?" Jackson asked. Liz never really told Jackson she had a date, but he was old enough to figure some things out on his own, so there was no need to ask him how he knew.

"Yeah, his name is Antoinne, I think you will like him. He should be here around five." Liz responded. "So, I want you to make sure your room is picked up and your bed is made" She added.

"I don't plan on inviting him in my room" Jackson replied in an irritated tone.

"Yeah well, you are still going to make your bed, please" she threw the please to make it sound more like a request than an order, but either way she expected the bed to be made. Liz began to brown the ground beef and spicy sausage for her sauce. She chopped onions, garlic, and mushrooms to sauté with the meat. It took a few hours to make the sauce and get the lasagna in the oven. She then prepared the salad and put it in the refrigerator. The table was set, and the wine was breathing. Everything was perfect except Liz, she was a wreck. She still had an hour to get showered. Liz washed with her favorite vanilla soap and applied lotion of the same scent. She was going for a more natural feel and look this evening. Just a relaxed Sunday night at home. She dressed in soft pink, casual but pretty. She had just finished applying a light coat of gloss when the doorbell rang. Jackson yelled "I'll get it." Liz decided to give them a moment to get acquainted before she went in to the living room. She approached Antoinne and gave him a small peck on the cheek. "Dinner smells great, and you look really nice" he smiled. She could see by the look on his face he wanted to kiss her but thought better of it with her son there.

"Thank you, I hope you like lasagna"

"I love it" he replied.

"So, Jackson" Antoinne began "What video games do you have? I was hoping we could play a game or two before dinner"

Liz smiled knowing this was certainly a sure way to get into her son's good graces.

"How about Madden? Do you want to play football?" Jackson asked.

"Cool, can you set it up?" Antoinne asked.

"Yeah sure I will go get it now" Jackson replied running toward his bedroom. When he slipped out of sight Antoinne moved in close to steel a quick kiss. "How am I supposed to keep my hands off of you when you look so beautiful?" He whispered pulling her body to his.

"Shh, he has ears like an elephant!" She giggled, kissing him passionately. Liz pulled away when she heard her son come out of his bedroom. "What can I get you to drink?" she asked.

"Water would be great Baby" he responded.

Liz listened to their small talk about video games and football while she pulled out the shrimp appetizer and poured Antoinne's drink. They devoured the shrimp and Liz set the table for dinner. When she finished, she sat down on the love seat next to Antoinne and watched them play the video football game. "See the wide receiver on my team? Number 37?" Jackson asked Antoinne. Liz sat up fast. She was giving her son the "I will step on your neck if you do it" look but he refused to turn and look back at her.

"Yeah, what about him?" Antoinne asked.

"My mom used to date him" Jackson replied. Liz took the couch pillow at threw it at the back of her son's head. Antoinne laughed.

"It's ok Sweetie" he said to her. "That's kind of cool that she dated a pro football player isn't it?" Antoinne asked.

"Well I never met him, they only went out a couple times, she said he was a jerk" Jackson replied.

"So, are you ready for dinner?" Liz turned toward Antoinne.

"Sure, can we pause the game?" He asked Jackson.

"Yeah, we can finish after dinner" Jackson replied.

Liz gave Jackson a raised eyebrow as they moved to the kitchen, he knew they would be having words later. The three of them sat down at the table together. Jackson began to tell Antoinne all about his football team. "I really don't get the playing time I should, but I love it anyway. Maybe you could come to one of my games?" Liz was thrilled her son was so open to Antoinne. "I am playing next weekend when we get back from Hilton Head, I am going to miss our game Saturday though, and my coach is really pissed." He announced.

"Hey language please!" Liz gave him the eye. She hated it when he used language like that, although she had been known to swear like a sailor when she was really angry, she didn't want her twelve-year-old following her example.

"Oh sorry" He said casually, not meaning it at all. Antoinne knew what Liz was thinking and gave her a little wink.

"This lasagna is the best I have ever had" Antoinne commented to Liz.

"Good, I made too much, you will have to take some home with you, or we will be eating it all week" She replied.

"Great, I will" he answered.

After dinner Jackson and Antoinne returned to the living room to finish their game while Liz cleaned up the kitchen. She enjoyed listening to them talk about sports, and she really appreciated his attempt to remind her son that sports are great but school comes first and his grades have to be his priority. Liz knew it was probably falling on deaf ears, but she liked that he was saying it. She finished loading the dishwasher and packed a plastic container of lasagna for Antoinne to take home. She asked if they were ready for dessert, both declined so Liz made a cup of tea and sat down on the loveseat near Antoinne and watched them play. He played the game as well as any twelve-year-old boy did, and Liz secretly wondered if that was perhaps a red flag. She smiled to herself as she couldn't help but think men are just boys in bigger bodies. When the game ended Jackson said he was going to head to his room, he had some reading to finish up, which Liz knew was code for he wanted to go text on the phone with his friends.

"He's a great kid, you've done a good job with him" Antoinne said as he pulled Liz close to her and kissed her softly on the mouth.

"Thank you, like I told you on the phone, his father isn't around, so it's just been the two of us. Sometimes he can be a real handful, but I can't imagine my life without him. He's my world."

"Yeah, I can tell." He said with a smile. "When do you leave on your business trip?" He asked.

"We fly out Thursday evening and back in Sunday early, afternoon. I will spend Monday and Tuesday writing my article and I will drop it off to my editor on Wednesday if all goes well." Liz answered.

"I wish I was going with you, I would enjoy making love to you on a beach under the stars" He said stroking her cheek.

"Honey, Hilton Head is still the south and if they see your black, naked ass on top of me they will shoot first and ask questions later! We better save that for a tropical island not South Carolina." They both laughed.

Antoinne pulled the zipper of her cotton jacket down slightly exposing her full cleavage and her matching lace bra.

"That's better" He said admiring the view. He leaned forward kissing her neck and breast area. Liz glanced at her watch 8:30pm. Liz knew it would be an hour still before Jackson went to sleep. She wanted Antoinne to undress her and make love to her right there but that wasn't an option with her son just down the hall.

"How about a movie?" Liz asked.

"Sure, sounds good." he answered, reading her mind. Liz walked over and pulled out a few movies for Antoinne to choose from. "Remember the Titans! I love this movie! How about this one?" He asked sounding a bit like a fourteen-year-old boy. Liz thought he was adorable.

"Sure, I like it too, it's Jackson's favorite. As soon as he hears the TV, he will be in here to watch it with us." She replied. As the movie began Liz grabbed her favorite throw and snuggled up next to Antoinne on the loveseat. She fit perfectly against his chest, his arm draped around her. Jackson heard the movie begin and made his way to the couch. "I love this movie!" He exclaimed. Both Jackson and Antoinne were glued to the television. Liz felt wonderful. This is what it's like, she thought. This is what it feels like to be a whole family. She was safe in the arms of a man she was falling in love with, her son was there too. It was the perfect moment, one that a single mother could truly appreciate. Antoinne and Jackson enjoyed talking about the movie, Liz was happy just to see them getting along so well. "How about dessert?" Liz asked.

"Sounds great mom!" Jackson replied.

"Sure Sweetie" Antoinne chimed in. Liz went to the kitchen and heated the apple pie, she added a couple scoops of vanilla ice cream to the top and served her two men their dessert in front of the television. They both thanked her but didn't really take their eyes off the television screen. Antoinne smiled devilishly as he fed a bite of his pie to Liz. "I love those lips" he whispered, sliding the spoon between them. Liz raised her eyebrows and glanced at Jackson who seemed completely oblivious to them. Finally, the movie ended. Jackson announced he was heading to bed. He kissed Liz goodnight and shook Antoinne's hand. "Nice meeting you" Jackson told Antoinne. Liz was glad he actually sounded like he meant it.

"Yeah you too, I'm looking forward to catching one of your games when you and your mom get back from Hilton Head." Antoinne replied.

"Cool, see ya" Jackson responded on his way to his room. Now that they were alone Liz cuddled in close to Antoinne. He leaned over and kissed her soft on her mouth. "I am gonna miss you while you are gone!" Antoinne said, sounding surprised. It was pretty obvious his feelings were developing as quickly as Liz's were.

"I feel the same way." She whispered looking into his eyes. They sat together on the sofa talking about their lives. Antoinne told Liz about his closest friends from childhood and college, Liz told him about Jenna. They talked about their families, they were both the oldest child. Liz asked him if his family would have a problem with her being white. "I don't think so, I think they just want me to be happy" he answered, but Liz could tell he wasn't completely convinced of that. "How about your family?" He asked.

"Well since my son is biracial, I think the cat is out of the bag." She responded laughingly. "Honestly, they don't care at all, they just want me to be with someone who is good to us." Liz purposely said "us" to make sure it was quite clear to Antoinne that she came as a package. Her son was just as much a part of this relationship as she was. Being a single mom didn't allow her to separate the two. Every man she dated had to be looked at as a potential father and role model for her son. Liz had gotten much pickier since her son was old enough to meet the men she dated. She seemed to hold a much higher standard for him than she had for herself in the past. "So why are you single?" Liz asked.

"I was in a relationship for a couple of years, we were actually engaged, but we argued all the time and just didn't seem to be on the same page. I think we both just decided it was time to move on." He answered. "What about you, why are you single and what's up with Jackson's dad?"

"Well he isn't around. He has bounced in and out of our lives over the years but when I closed myself down and stopped allowing him to have an on again off again relationship with me, he stopped coming over. Jackson hasn't seen or heard from him in over a year now."

"Wow" Antoinne replied. Liz knew there was no point in sugar coating things, she needed to be honest with him if she wanted them to have a chance.

"Anyway" she continued "I have been in a couple long term relationships when Jackson was too young to notice and in the past few years, I haven't really been involved with anyone because I just haven't had the time or any real interest. I have been focused on my career and raising my son. I don't want him to grow up remembering men coming and going and spending the night with his mother. I would never just expose him like that."

"You are really good with him." Antoinne said, stroking her face.

"Thank you, it's not easy and we have had some rough moments, but I try." Liz answered. "It's important to me to make sure you understand right from the beginning that my son is the most important thing in my life. I won't be with anyone who has no interest in being in his life as well as mine. We come as a package. I don't think that means you have to jump through hoops for his approval, but it is important to me that any man I date understand that his needs come first."

"I get that." Antoinne answered. "I think he's a great kid and I am looking forward to getting to know him better."

Liz hugged him tighter. She wondered if this could really be happening. Was this guy as amazing as he seemed to be? Antoinne pulled her chin up to look in her eyes. "I'm falling for you " he whispered as he kissed her mouth. They sat snuggled on the couch talking. He stroked her hair and they discussed their past, and their dreams for the future. The conversation was easy, and the chemistry was amazing. An hour had passed before Liz tiptoed down the hall to check and see if Jackson was asleep. She could see him snoring from the door. She came back to the living room and reached for Antoinne's hand. She led them to her bedroom. He shut and locked the door. She reached for the buttons on his shirt and slowly began to undress him. Liz knew if she wasn't in love with him, yet she certainly would be by the time she awoke in the morning. Antoinne slowly and carefully undressed her. Taking his time admiring every inch and curve of her body. The way he looked at her hungrily and with such desire removed every ounce of self-doubt she had. She could see in his eyes that he thought she was beautiful. He wanted her like she hadn't been wanted in a long time. He lowered his mouth to hers, kissing her softly and gently. Their bodies fell into her bed, intertwined together. She awoke to Antoinne getting dressed, glancing at the alarm clock the numbers glared 5:30am in bright red. "Wow, it's early" she whispered.

"Yeah, I need to be gone before your son wakes up and figures out, I spent the night with his mama. He might try and kick my ass." Antoinne whispered.

"Good point, thank you" Liz said rubbing her eyes and trying to sit up.

"Baby go back to sleep, I will let myself out." He said leaning over and kissing her gently.

"Ok, we'll have a great day" She said as she rolled over to go back to sleep. Liz wasn't really a morning person and needed a couple more hours of sleep before she could find her social graces. Two hours later she was drinking her Starbucks, nonfat, latte and driving Jackson to school. "Is there anything you need for the trip to Hilton Head?" She asked trying to focus on something other than the tightening in her chest. Earlier in the shower as Liz was washing her hair, it hit her. She knew she was in love with Antoinne. She felt excited, terrified, horrified, and sick to her stomach. How did this happen so fast? Why did she wear her heart on her sleeve like some fifteen-year-old school girl? There was no stopping it now. She was eating, drinking and breathing this man every moment of her day. Yeah, this tight feeling in her chest was not going to be leaving anytime soon.

"Nope, I don't need anything, what time do we fly out?" Jackson asked.

"I will pick you up from school and we will go straight to the airport on Thursday. The flight is only a couple of hours so we will be checked into our hotel in time to see the sunset at the beach." Liz answered as she pulled into the school parking lot.

"Cool" he replied as he leaned over and gave his mother a quick peck on the cheek before bailing out of the car. "See ya", he called over his shoulder as he hurried to meet up with his friends.

"Have a great day" Liz replied, half of which was said after the door shut. Liz drove toward the University hospital. She was picking up the research notes she needed to write for the two informational pamphlets for the physician services department. One was on acne and a new skin care trial for teens, the other on sexually transmitted diseases and the importance of getting tested. Liz really preferred writing travel articles for magazines but these were simple assignments that helped pay the bills. She knew she could get them both done before she left for South Carolina if she got started right away. After collecting the notes and the assignment outline from the hospital Liz returned home and began writing. She was grateful for the distraction, she needed to focus on something other than the fact that she was falling in love. She had plowed through a full pot of coffee and was more than halfway finished with the first article when the doorbell rang. Liz peeked out the window but all she could see was the back end of a white van in her driveway. She opened her front door to delivery man holding a large vase of pink flowers. "Oh wow" Liz muttered.

"I have a delivery for Liz Butler" the young man announced.

"That would be me" She answered.

"Here you go ma'am, have a nice day" he said handing her flowers and disappearing before she could say "thank you".

Liz inhaled the beautiful bouquet. It was filled with a variety of pink flowers. Pink Gerber Daisies, Pink Hydrangeas, Pink Tulips, pink flowers she didn't know the names of. Liz set the vase on the counter and opened the card.

It said "Hope these bring a smile to your beautiful face, Xoxo, Antoinne" Liz reached for her phone and dialed his number.

"Hi Sexy" he answered.

"Thank you so much for the beautiful flowers" She said softly.

"I'm glad you like them" he replied.

"I love them" She answered. "I just saw you this morning and I miss you already. What have you done to me?" she asked.

"I feel the same way, I miss you whenever I am not with you" he said in an almost whisper, as if he was afraid to say it aloud. "I'm not letting you leave without seeing you again" he said as a matter of fact.

"Well Jackson has a game Wednesday night, it's a make-up from a game that was rained out, would you like to go with me?"

"I would love to" he replied. "I will call you later tonight." he answered.

"Ok and thank you again the flowers are really beautiful" she said.

"So are you, talk you tonight" and he hung up the phone.

Chapter 5

By the time Thursday arrived Liz wasn't sure how she would be able to stand being away from Antoinne for even a few days. She had fallen asleep in his arms the past four nights, so she wondered how she supposed to just get on a plane and leave now for a long weekend away from him? She called her best friend on the way to pick up Jackson from school.
"Jenna I am so in love with him it scares me!" Liz whined into the receiver.
"Hey Pal, I was wondering when you were going to come up for air and call me, I haven't heard from you all week." Jenna responded in a slightly annoyed tone.
"That is because he has been here every night. It's been amazing. He and Jackson are totally hitting it off. He is everything I have ever wanted. He is smart and sexy, and I swear we lay awake all night talking. We talk about everything. I have opened up to him like I have never opened up to anyone. I am in love with him Pal, completely and totally in love with him in and if it's a dream then I hope I never wake up because I have never been this happy in my life. I actually like getting up and making him breakfast! I like packing his lunch and writing little love notes on the napkins for Christ sake! I am June Fucking Cleaver. What is happening to me? I never thought I would let anyone this close to me again. I have known him ten minutes and I am head over heels! Please tell me how to make it stop because I feel like I am on the edge of the most beautiful cliff in the world." Liz said without taking a breath.
"Wow, well you have never been one to move slowly. It's a trait we share Pal, I don't have a clue as to how to slow it down. I don't know how to balance love with logic. I am just like you are, I dive in without knowing the depth of the water and usually it means I get my spine crushed when my head it's the bottom, so I am the last person on earth who can tell you how to slow it down." Jenna responded.
"I'm scared of being so happy" Liz whispered. "I have never in my life thought this was possible, Jackson's dad is just such a jerk and the more time I spend with Antoinne the more I realize how much was missing in my relationship with him. Antoinne is not just my amazing, well hung, lover he is my friend. He encourages me, he is compliments me, he thinks I am brilliant and beautiful, and no man has ever thought that about me before."
"Well I knew he had to be well hung, or you wouldn't be in love" Jenna replied as both women laughed out loud. "Second, this is what falling in love is supposed to be like Pal, it's supposed to be with a man who thinks the sun revolves around you. You are just so use to dating assholes you have forgotten what nice guys are like." Jenna said as a matter of fact.
"God, I am so scared it's gonna all come crashing down, ya know?" Liz said sounding like a young girl instead of a thirty-seven-year-old woman. "We haven't been apart in days, now I have to get on the plane for Hilton Head and leave him for four days. I think I need it. I think I need a few days to get my head on straight and think this through, a little distance will help that I guess, it's happening so fast. I am terrified, Jackson is getting attached to him to, and you know I never bring men around him, I hope and pray I am not making a huge mistake."
"You aren't" Jenna said adamantly. "Jackson is a strong, resilient kid and no matter what happens he will be great, so don't even worry about that part of it. See what happens while you are gone. Let him miss you a little, it's good for him. He will be thinking about you and calling you the whole time you are there, I am sure of it."

"I gave him a drawer." Liz tossed in casually.

"Holy shit you gave him a drawer?" Jenna said mockingly.

"Well technically it's two drawers, I gave him the nightstand."

"My God please tell me you haven't picked out a damn dress yet!" Jenna teased.

"Oh, shut up Bitch, I will marry him just to make you wear a big, puffy, lavender dress with a million ruffles and a hoop skirt" Liz teased.

"And I would wear it just for you Pal." Jenna said sweetly.

"That's why I love you, I will call you from Hilton Head, Jackson is walking up now, and we are headed straight to the airport"

"Ok, be safe, talk to you soon, bye" Jenna said before disconnecting.

Jackson climbed into the backseat of the SUV. "Hi Sweetie, did you have a good day?" Liz asked.

"Yeah it was good, are we going straight to the airport now?" Jackson asked.

"Yes, by the time we get there, get parked and go through security it will be time to board." She replied. Liz hated flying and Jackson knew it. She loved to go places but hated the flying part. They made it through security and to the gate with twenty minutes to spare. Liz grabbed a bottle of water for herself and a soda for Jackson. She needed to take a Xanax before boarding or she would have an anxiety attack during takeoff. "Just a little something to take the edge off." She thought before popping the little white pill into her mouth and taking a large gulp of water to help her swallow. Ten minutes later they were seated on the plane and Liz was as relaxed as she could be and still be awake. Jackson had his iPod on and was watching all the action on the runway. Liz leaned back in her seat and shut her eyes. Two hours later Jackson shook her arm. "Mom we are landing." He whispered. "You totally started to snore, I had to shut your mouth once." He said completely horrified.

Liz opened her eyes and reached into her purse for the bottle of water. Alright, perhaps she was a little too relaxed from the Xanax. A good, strong cup of coffee would have her feeling refreshed and ready to go. They stepped off the plane with their carry-on bags in tow. She had learned to pack lightly for these weekend trips. Liz saw the Starbucks stand just outside of the gate. She ordered a nonfat latte and drank it on the way to find the rental car counter, she certainly didn't want to be driving around a strange city with her head in a Xanax fog. Half way through the cup she was feeling human again. The rental car company was out of mid-size sedans and gave them a free upgrade which turned out to be a little, red convertible. Jackson was thrilled to be in a car with the top down. Liz tried to share in her son's enthusiasm, but she knew this would mean she would look like "The Wreck of the Hesperus" as her grandmother would say. Liz had surmised "The Wreck of the Hesperus" was story of a shipwreck that couldn't have been pretty because whenever Grandma referred to someone looking like "The Wreck of the Hesperus" it was usually really, really bad. Liz used her sunglasses as a hair band to keep her from being blinded by it while they drove the forty-five minutes with the top down from the airport to The Sea Pines Plantation on Hilton Head. Sea Pines is a resort area located at the southern tip of the island. Guests were only allowed in by pass and if you weren't staying in the community you had to pay to enter. It was gated and monitored by round the clock security. Once behind the gate you saw true southern charm at its finest. The homes were all replicated in the same muted shades of earth tones, which she knew was a community requirement. The big, beautiful trees lining the streets dripped in Spanish Moss, this immediately caught Jackson's eye as they didn't have anything like it in Michigan. "What is that?" he asked. Just as she finished explaining to him that he shouldn't touch it, as its harbored bugs, they spotted a small alligator near the side of the road. "Wow! Look at that!" He screamed. Regardless of what the natives said Liz would never get comfortable with alligators just wandering around freely. Liz and Jackson both agreed that the Sea Pines area was beautiful, and it seemed like a cross between northern Michigan and Florida. She couldn't help but wish Antoinne was there with them. They arrived at The Inn at Harbour Town just after six. Liz knew they would need to hurry if they wanted to catch the sunset. Sea Pines was one of the popular resort areas for tourists and golfers. It was hard to call it a resort though since it takes up over five thousand acres which is about a third of the island. Liz thought it was better described as the most distinct of the four neighborhoods on the island. It boasts huge pine trees and Liz was amazed to learn people actually buy the pine needles from the area to add to their landscaping at home. There was so much humidity in the air that everything felt damp to the touch and smelled earthy. The resort also housed three championship golf courses and hosted the Heritage PGA golf tournament each spring. All of this and the beautiful beach of the Atlantic made it easy to see why this a favorite vacation spot for family's generation after generation. It maintained its charm with subtle nuances and old-fashioned bicycles. No one really used a car much in the resort area, everyone rode bicycles. "The bicycle may be a challenge." Liz said to Jackson as they waited for a family of five to ride their bikes across the path before, they could pull into the resort.

"How long since you have been on a bike mom?" Jackson asked.

"I am guessing it's been about twenty years." She said with a bit of concern.

"Oh boy" he said with the same shadow of concern. "I guess we better make sure you get a helmet then." He snickered. Liz knew the article would pretty much write itself as the area was so beautiful. They checked into their three-bedroom villa, since it is one of the most popular rentals. They dropped their bags and headed straight to the beach which was just a short walk away. Jackson spotted the lighthouse and added that to their list of things to do for the next day. "Yeah climbing a million steps sounds like a great time." She teased. The sky was a beautiful pink hue. The tide had come in and there was a strong breeze blowing. The beach wasn't typical of something you would see in Florida or the Caribbean. It had tall sea grasses and pine trees along the shore. It was truly spectacular. Jackson ran down the boardwalk he kicked off his shoes and immediately put his toes in the water. Liz was busy snapping pictures of the pink sky where it joined the ocean. They spread out a blanket and sat with her arm around the shoulder of her baby boy watching the sun disappear into the horizon. "It's beautiful here" he commented.

Liz was really wishing Antoinne was sitting on the blanket with them watching the sun go down. She wanted him to be wrapped around her, sheltering her from the cold and taking in the beauty of their surroundings. She pulled out her phone to check the time and saw she had a missed text message from Antoinne. It said, "Wow I miss you already and I wish I was there with you."

Liz text back "I feel the same way, not sure how I will sleep tonight without you here to keep me safe." Once the sunset she and Jackson headed out to find a place to have dinner. After dinner at the Crazy Crab they walked over to Scoops for ice cream cones and then headed back to their villa they were both exhausted. Even though she was missing Antoinne, Liz was really enjoying spending time alone with Jackson. She couldn't imagine her existence without him. He was truly her whole life and every time she thought about him growing up and leaving her to make his own way in the world, she felt like she might slip into a black hole of loneliness. Jackson went straight to bed completely exhausted. Liz took a quick shower, put on her favorite lotion, and her light blue, cotton pajamas then crawled into bed to dial Antoinne. He picked up on the second ring. "Hi Baby." She could hear the excitement in his voice over her call.

"Hi Sunshine, how are you?" She asked.

"Better now, how are you? Was your flight ok?" He asked.

"Well I guess, I slipped into a Xanax coma and Jackson woke me when we were landing." They both laughed.

She filled him in on the details of their evening and he told her how much he wished he was there with her. They stayed on the phone for over an hour talking about everything and nothing at all. Finally, when Liz couldn't keep her eyes open anymore, she said goodnight. She was so exhausted she said "I love you" without even thinking about it, as if she had said it a million times before. Realizing after the fact what she had done she sat up quickly, her heart racing like a speeding train. "Oh Shit" she thought to herself. She then began talking rapidly and nonsensically to fill the air with anything. He pretended not to notice and let her continue to ramble without comment. "So, call me tomorrow, I need to get some rest, Jackson wants to climb to the top of the lighthouse first thing in the morning." Liz said without breathing. "Sweet dreams." She threw in as an afterthought and hung up the phone before he could say anything. She immediately dialed Jenna.

"It's after eleven on a work night, this better be important" she said answering the phone.

"I was talking to Antoinne and I was getting sleepy and I accidentally said I love you without even thinking about it. Then I rambled like the village idiot without even giving him a chance to process it and hung up the phone." Liz blurted out.

"Oh Jesus." Jenna said quietly.

"I know right????" Liz screamed! "What in the Sam hell am I going to do now? I probably just sent him running and he will never call me again. You know he is thinking how in the hell is this crazy bitch in love with me after two weeks? Damn!" Liz was now pacing around her bedroom.

"Ok, well don't panic, tomorrow if he calls tell him you had been drinking at dinner if he brings it up." Jenna offered.

"Yeah that isn't going to work, we had been talking for an hour before I let the L bomb drop and he knows I wasn't drunk!" Liz bellowed in the phone.

"Well Pal, I guess I would just pretend it didn't happen, let it be the giant, white elephant in the room for a while." Jenna suggested.

"Great, that will be comfortable for both of us" Liz was ready to cry. At thirty-seven years old if she knew one thing at all it was that saying, I love you to a man first was a mortal sin and saying it after only knowing him a couple weeks made her not only stupid but crazy. Yeah, he was probably deleting her number out of his phone right now. Best case scenario he knew he had her on lock down now and could get anything and everything he wanted from her. "How can one stupid, fucking word change everything forever?" Liz was in a full-blown melt down.

"Ok Pal, you need to take a deep breath. It isn't the end of the world. You two have been spending every minute you can together and it's going to be fine, he clearly has some pretty strong feelings for you. You need to relax. Just calm down. If that sends him running, then it wasn't going to last very long, and you may as well know it now." Jenna said logically.

"You are right, but damn I wish I could go back in time fifteen minutes and suck that right back in." Liz said sounding defeated. "Well you need to get some sleep so I will let you go, I am going to go cry myself to sleep now."

"Jesus, you are being dramatic, it's going to be fine. Just get some rest and call me tomorrow."

"I will, goodnight." Liz said hanging up her cell phone. She tossed and turned for an hour trying to figure out a way to take back the "I love you" but there was nothing she could do. Bringing it up would only make things more awkward and uncomfortable. Jenna was right, it was better to leave it alone and let it be the big, white elephant in the room.

The next morning Liz and Jackson had breakfast and headed out to explore the lighthouse in Harbour Town. It was a lot of steps, but the view was amazing. They explored the shops next to the Lighthouse and bought a few souvenirs to take home. Liz found a t shirt for Antoinne. As she paid for it, she wondered if she was even going to see him again. Liz knew she was probably overreacting, but it was something she did well. Whenever a crisis of any kind occurred, she could be counted on to over react. She hated that quality in herself and tried to no avail to correct this little character flaw of hers. She was emotional, hot tempered and dramatic. These qualities were both her strengths and her weaknesses. Without them she would have never achieved her career success or survived single parenthood, but sometimes she was her own worst enemy and she said things without thinking. She had a fierce tongue and had been known on occasion to cut a person to shreds with it. She preferred to think of herself as passionate instead of crazy. Her passion about every aspect of life drew people to her. She took chances, she was brilliant and brave, and life didn't scare her. She didn't let people tell her no, it wasn't even in her vocabulary.

Her phone rang, she saw Antoinne's name appear on the screen of her cell phone. Her heart dropped into her stomach. "Hello" she said softly.

"Well good morning Sexy, how did you sleep?" He asked.

"Great, I think it's the ocean air." She responded trying to act casual.

He asked about Jackson and talked about the sites they were planning on seeing that day. He was in good spirits and there was no mention of the disaster the night before. "I really miss you, what time do you come home on Sunday?" He questioned.

"We land at three, so we will be home by four or so" She responded.

"Great, how about I come by at six and I'll bring dinner?" Antoinne suggested.

"I didn't know you could cook." Liz questioned.

"I can't, I will just pick up something if that's ok." He asked.

"That would be really nice." She answered.

"Ok well tell Jackson I said hi and enjoy your day I will call you tonight." He said wrapping up their conversation.

"Sounds good, bye" she said hanging up the phone. She didn't know if she should be thrilled, he didn't mention their conversation and her dropping the L bomb on him or irritated that he was just ignoring it. Liz decided to let it go, she was going to enjoy the rest of the weekend with her son. They spent the afternoon exploring the different beaches on the island. They went to the South Beach area and then left the Sea Pines to check out the parts of the island. First stop was the Palmetto Dunes where they caught a ride on a dune buggy down the three mile stretch of beach. Liz found a beautiful spot in the sand to take notes for her article while Jackson took a surfing lesson. The water was a little rough, but he was picking it up quickly, he had a lot of athletic ability and seemed to excel at everything he did, not a skill he had acquired from her. She snapped a few great pictures of him balancing on his board. He was having a great time. She felt so blessed to be able to do these things for her son. Liz offered

up a quiet prayer of thanks for all the amazing blessings she had in her life. She wasn't particularly religious, but she was spiritual and truly believed in a higher power. She knew she had so many things to be thankful for. They returned to Sea Pines late in the afternoon. Jackson wanted to take a short nap before they went to dinner. A couple hours later they headed out to the Old Oyster Factory for dinner. It was known for its amazing views of the lowlands. Liz had the scallops and Jackson ordered the fried seafood dinner. They talked about the surf lessons, Jackson told her it reminded him a lot of the first time he went snowboarding except it was like the ground kept moving. She loved his animation as he re-lived his experience for her. "I wish we lived on the ocean" he commented.
"Sometimes I do too, but it gets too hot and humid here, we would be ready to faint by the time July rolled around." Liz responded.
"Well then maybe we need one place in Michigan for the summers and one in the south for the winters." Jackson had found the solution.
"Yeah that would be great! Maybe when we win the lottery." She laughed. Just as they were finishing dinner Liz's cell phone rang. "It's Antoinne she announced to Jackson.
"Cool can I answer it I want to tell him about my surf lesson today." Jackson said excitedly. Liz handed her son the phone and listened to her son retell the story of how sweet he thought surfing was to Antoinne. He told him about the beach and the villa and how awesome the trip was. Liz enjoyed listening to him talk. She was so happy they were developing such a bond, even though on some level it still terrified her a little.
The next day they checked out every public beach on the island and then decided to go horseback riding. Liz didn't really love animals, she tried but she just couldn't understand the bond people shared with a creature that smelled bad and left its hair everywhere. She didn't feel a special bond toward cats or dogs, she thought birds were basically rats with wings and belonged outside. She certainly didn't think she would suddenly develop a strong bond with a horse but since her son really wanted them to do it, she decided she could give it a try. Jackson had ridden a horse at summer camp a few times, but Liz hadn't been on since she was a child. She was pretty sure this would end up being thrown from the horse and go home on crutches or with a closed head injury but luckily the horse she was on was too old and too slow to do any real damage. On the plane ride home Jackson told his mom what a great time he had with her. She agreed the trip had been perfect but she was anxious for the plane to land in Detroit so they could get home. She had missed Antoinne so much she couldn't wait to see him.

Chapter 6

When Liz arrived home with Jackson, they unloaded the car and Jackson headed straight to get dressed for his Sunday night practice, his coach was not happy he had missed a game for this trip, and he was a little stressed about the extra laps he may end up running. Liz assured him he would not be punished and she had cleared everything with his coach but she could see he was still anxious and decided she would sit in the stands at practice just to make sure he knew she was there and to collar his coach should there be any repercussions, this was not the NFL, it was not even high school ball yet, as far as she was concerned it was perfectly fine to miss an occasional game, and since this was the first time he had ever missed a game in over his six years of playing she did not see any harm in it. She sent Antoinne a text and told him they were home safe and that she needed to stay at practice with Jackson just because he seemed a little anxious so she would call him later. They arrived at practice and Jackson took his place on the field for warm ups and Liz headed to the bleachers with a blanket and a cup of decaf to watch. He was doing great, working hard and showing his coach that he was anxious to make up for lost time. She was so proud of him. His worth ethic and dedication made her heart feel like it would burst out of her chest, for a brief moment she had a quick flash of hate toward his father for missing this moment and so many others just like it. There was no place else Liz would rather be than right where she was, watching this beautiful boy of hers doing what he loved.

Liz looked up to see Antoinne walking across the track that circled the field toward her, carrying a dozen red roses. Liz was shocked. She had no idea he would drive out and meet them at practice. He walked up the bleachers and sat down next to her. Antoinne gave her the beautiful flowers, kissed her cheek and whispered "I love you too" in her ear. Liz felt tears welling up in her eyes. She couldn't cry at football practice, Jackson would be horrified! She swallowed hard and squeezed his hand and put her head on his shoulder. She could not be any happier than she was at this very moment. Her beautiful boy, happy and doing what he loves and this amazing man next to her just told her he loved her. Life had never been so good.

Antoinne was very interested in watching practice. It was clear to Liz he wanted to be out on the field coaching him. He moved down to the sideline and gave Jackson a few tips. He edged closer and closer and began a conversation on the sidelines with the coaches. The next thing Liz knew Antoinne was pointing to the field and calling out plays. Liz laughed and shook her head, looks like he wormed his way into a coaching spot. Jackson was beaming with pride as the coaches seemed excited to have Antoinne's help and liked his ideas. Jackson stepped up and worked even harder to make sure he showed Antoinne his skills and talent. Liz loved that this was something they could share. She didn't know nearly as much about the sport as she should for someone who has spent as many hours on the sidelines as she had but she still loved watching him play. Rain or shine, sun or snow, it did not matter, she would be there cheering and praying.

After practice they went out for chili dogs and milkshakes and headed home to hit the showers. Jackson was showered and fed and asleep before his head hit the pillow. Liz was exhausted from their full day. Antoinne turned on the Sunday night football game, after all it was never ending at this time of year and Liz put her flowers in a vase and then took a bubble bath, she was careful to put on lotion and she slipped into a pink, silk nightshirt and nothing else. When they finally crawled into bed together Liz couldn't wait to put her arms around him and just be next to him. She had missed him while they were in Hilton Head and she slept so much better when he was wrapped around her. "That was a great game, the Lions pulled off the win in the last two minutes!" Antoinne exclaimed with excitement as he pulled off his shirt and tossed it to the floor. "I am going to jump in the shower" he said as Liz watched him remove his clothes. She loved every hard inch of his chocolate brown body. He was in excellent shape. His lean frame was solid and well defined, every muscle outlined. She loved to just look at him, he was beautiful and if she thought about it too hard, she would begin to feel insecure about what he was doing with her. She knew such a handsome, successful man could choose any woman he wanted but for some reason he chose her, and she was trying desperately not to pick it apart and doubt herself or his love. He emerged from the shower, turned off the lights and crawled naked into the bed they shared most nights. Antoinne lowered himself over Liz and kissed her gently. "I missed you so much" He whispered. "What have you done to me?' He asked

"I told you I am magic!" Liz laughed and kissed him. "You belong to me now" she said only half joking and pulled him to her closer. Antoinne kissed her harder, his hands caressed her hair and stroked her face, pulling her neck toward him he began to devour her mouth and working his way down her chest. Liz clearly belonged to him too and he knew it. She arched her back welcoming his soft lips and tongue as they teased and sucked her nipples and moved down her stomach. His gentle kisses nurtured her soul and tortured her body. His teeth gently bit into her hip as she rocked them toward him, encouraging him to go further. He teased her and taunted her with his mouth not giving her what he knew she wanted yet. Antoinne moved his lips to her thighs running his tongue along the insides of her legs to her hips, purposely tormenting her. Liz attempted to guide his head between her legs. "Please" she whispered.

"Tell me you love me." His husky voice demanded as he pinned her arms to her side.

"I love you, I am falling so fast and so hard for you, it scares the hell out of me" Liz whispered. Pleading for him to give her what she so desperately needed. With that he slid his tongue inside of her, Liz cried out in ecstasy. His lips and tongue delicately licking her and stroking her to climax, Liz cried out as her body shuddered and tried to pull away but Antoinne held her arms tightly not allowing her to move as he drove himself fast and hard inside of her. Liz's body came up off the bed and rolled on top of him, her hips moving up and down as his hands guided her in perfect rhythm. Liz leaned over Antoinne dropping her milky white breast into his mouth. Harder and harder his body pounded into hers. She couldn't breathe. Liz again felt her body tighten. "Oh God baby now, please now" she muttered softly. Faster and faster.

"Now? You want it now?" He teased.

"Yes, I am begging, now" Liz could barely say the words as the intensification of her orgasm mounted. Finally, Antoinne exploded deep inside of her. Liz collapsed on top of him, trying desperately to catch her breath and her body gently shook. Antoinne wrapped his arms around her and held her tight. "God, I love you" he said softly.

"I love you too and remind me of that when I can't walk tomorrow" they both laughed as she curled into his chest and fell asleep, happier than she had ever been.

Chapter 7

"Tonight, Antoinne and I are going downtown. We haven't been to Detroit for a while and I really want to go to the casino." Liz told Jenna as she balanced the phone with her shoulder and washed the dishes Jackson had left in the sink.

"It's our ten-month anniversary, I can't believe we have been together almost a year. Oh, and we closed on that house I was telling you about, so we are celebrating that too. It needs a lot of work but it's in one of the better neighborhoods in Detroit and I think we can make a nice profit off of flipping it. I am excited for us to do it together too. I am really enjoying doing the flips with him. I am so glad he talked me into getting my real estate license. We made twenty-eight thousand off that little bungalow and we only had it for two months. I love it. I love searching the web for great deals and driving around looking at houses with him. Tomorrow Jackson is going to go with Antoinne and start gutting the place." Liz admitted there had been some adjustments in the beginning when Antoinne first moved in with her and Jackson in November but overall it had been wonderful. Jackson wasn't always thrilled to have a man around the house. There were certain cultural differences in the way they were raised, Liz knew black parents tended to be stricter with their children so sometimes they disagreed, but she was grateful for his input. He was there to help with Jackson's homework, throw the ball around, and most importantly to make him to be respectful and teach him all the things he needed to know about being a man. He did it in a way a father does with his son and their relationship had quickly turned into that. Liz knew she had found her soulmate. He was everything she needed. Their life was good, and she was the perfect housewife. Well the perfect house wife who wasn't really any one's wife. She wondered if Antoinne really had any intentions of proposing to her. She knew he loved her, but it wasn't easy for him to say it. In fact, in their ten months together she could count on one hand how many times he had said the actual words. Two of those times they were naked, so she wasn't sure if it even counted. Generally naked "I love yous" mean something entirely different and any woman over the age of twenty-five knew as much. "I think we are going to the MGM Grand, you and Marybeth should meet us there, I haven't seen you in forever." Liz suggested.

"I would love to, but I will have to call you back and let you know after Marybeth gets home." Jenna replied.

"Antoinne doesn't love the casino like I do so I know he won't be thrilled to go but I am feeling lucky so I am hoping I can at least convince him to hang out there for a couple hours." Liz added.

"So is this guy going to make an honest woman of you, it's been almost a year. Has he mentioned marriage at all?" Jenna was reading her mind. She knew her best friend needed the whole perfect picture and had dreamed of an island wedding for as long as she could remember.

"The only time it even comes up is jokingly when I give him the best sex of his life." Liz said sounding slightly defeated. "Do you think I should bring it up or just leave it alone?" She asked.

"Well I think by Christmas if you don't have ring on your finger you will need to figure out if you can be happy leaving it the way it is or if you need to be married. You are basically living like you are married now." Jenna added.

"I know but honestly I am not sure he looks at me like someone he wants to marry. I still haven't met his parents. I know they live in Georgia, but his grandmother is here, and frankly we have been together close to a year now it seems like at some point he would mention us going to Georgia together to see his family." She said sounding concerned. "But on the other hand, he isn't close to his family like I am mine. He doesn't even talk to them once a week. I talk to my mom and sister every single day, so I see it differently I think."

"Well just wait and see what he says about the holidays this year. Maybe he is concerned they won't be alright with you being white and having a child." Jenna replied.

"I think that is probably a big part of it. He won't come right out and say it, but I know he and his grandmother had words over me being white and five years older than he is." Liz added.
"Seriously? I didn't realize that."

"Yeah, he was really upset and didn't elaborate, he mentioned that he called his mother over it because he never thought his Christian, equal rights preaching, sitting on the board of the church, grandmother could express such narrow minded and racist views. When I tried to question him about it, he shut me down and said he didn't want to discuss it. I just love being thought of as the white, devil whore by people who have never even met me." Liz said exasperated.

"That's always fun. Jenna said. She hated that Liz was being hurt by people who had never even taken the time to get to know her. "But Antoinne loves you and I don't think he will let anyone disrespect you at all. I am sure he would immediately step in and handle it." She added.

"I don't ever want it to come to that. I don't ever want Antoinne to have to choose between me and his family. I love him and frankly what they think of me is irrelevant, I couldn't care any less, but it will hurt him if they make this hard." Liz's heart grew heavy when she thought about it. "Maybe that's not it, what if he just doesn't feel like I am worth meeting them? What if he doesn't love me enough to take it to that level?" She asked.

"Well I don't think he would be living with you and playing daddy to Jackson if he didn't love you, that's just ridiculous." Jenna replied.

"I guess. I am just gonna leave it alone for now but yeah if Christmas comes and goes without a ring then I am going to need to reevaluate. In fact, if Christmas comes and goes without a ring, I'm gonna need to kick his ass to the curb!" Both women laughed, and both knew she loved him so much at this point that the chances of her ever being able to ask him to leave were slim and none. Liz's phone beeped. "Hang on I have another call." She said to Jenna. "Oh, it's Antoinne, call me when Marybeth gets home if you two want to meet us at the casino."

"Yeah ok I will, talk to you in a bit." Jenna said before hanging up.

"Hi Baby" Liz said as she answered his call.

"Hi Sweetie, how's your day going?" He asked.

"It's good I was just talking to Jenna, I told her we were going out to celebrate our anniversary and the new house tonight and that maybe they could meet us downtown at the MGM. Is that ok with you?"

"Sure, Baby I don't care, is Jackson still spending the night at his friends?" He asked.

"Yeah he is, so we don't have to worry about a thing." She replied.

"Good then pack a bag, let's stay downtown. Then we can have a nice dinner and a few drinks, and we don't have to worry about the drive home. I will call and get us a room at the casino. Can you pack for both of us, oh and make sure you include something red and sexy."?

"Honey, I don't think you have anything red and sexy." Liz mocked.

"I want you in that red dress and heels with the matching lace thong underneath." He ordered.

"Yes, Daddy." Liz laughed. She liked looking pretty for him. She had never really been the thong type before him but since he liked it so much, she was happy to accommodate his request, even if it did make her totally self-conscious to go into public wearing one. She knew it was ridiculous, no one knew what kind of panties she was wearing but in the back of her mind the whole world had x-ray vision and was horrified at her less than toned ass in a thong,

"Good girl." He teased. "Be ready at six, I will be home to grab a quick shower and we can head out the door. We can get checked into the room, have dinner and then do a little gambling since I know how much you love it."

"Ok Baby I will be ready when you get here. Bye" Liz replied before hanging up her cell. She called Jenna back and told her their plans just in case she wanted to meet up at the casino later. Then Liz packed their bags, she made sure to include her new red baby doll nightie. Antoinne loved her in red so that was her plan tonight. Head to toe red. She showered, put on his favorite perfume, a red lace bra, and matching thong. She wore the red knit wrap dress that showed just the right amount of cleavage and gave her a nice waistline. Liz decided to straighten her hair and put on a little extra makeup for the occasion. She looked pretty good she thought, the gold pumps were a little high, but she knew Antoinne would love them.

 Women had been sacrificing comfort for sexy over centuries now, one more night certainly wouldn't kill her. Antoinne pulled in at ten minutes after six. He was always late, Liz hadn't really expected to see him until closer to six thirty. "Hi Baby." She said as she walked to the door to greet him with a kiss.

"You look beautiful." He said, and he meant it. Antoinne couldn't deny how strongly he felt for her, it was all over his face every time she walked into the room.

"Thank you so much." Liz said beaming. This man had given her more confidence in herself than she had ever felt. He encouraged her. He was proud of her. He thought she was beautiful and brilliant, and she had never felt so special and so loved in her life. Liz hoped and prayed this feeling never went away. "I laid out your clothes on the bed. The green cashmere sweater and your Gerbeau jeans, is that ok? If not, I can iron a different shirt while you are in the shower." She offered. Liz knew their rolls were incredibly traditional, but she loved it. She liked cooking and cleaning and ironing for him. She liked that he was a real man and opened her doors and took care of the bills and handled all the things she grew up thinking men were supposed to handle. As far as Liz was concerned, she loved her career, but she was happy with her 1950's relationship. They both knew and enjoyed their rolls in it. Liz didn't care what the world thought. This whole feminist movement had done nothing but make life harder on women and ruin the American family. Most of the people in her world would be stunned to hear her say such a thing especially since she was so successful, but she wished she could have found her success more on her own terms. She wished that more women had the luxury of raising their own children instead of having them raised in day care centers. She wished the women's movement didn't give men an excuse to bail on their responsibilities.

"No Baby, thank you the green sweater and jeans are great. Did you pack everything we needed?" He asked.

"Yep I sure did." She smiled and gave him a little wink.

"Ok I will be ready in ten minutes then." He said heading to the shower.

When they arrived at the casino Antoinne got their room key and Liz found a slot machine.

"You can just keep playing Sweetie I will take our bag up to our room and come back and get you for dinner." He said kissing her on the forehead.

"Great, I will be right here, hurry back." Liz answered sliding a twenty into the machine.

Antoinne headed to the elevator, he had arranged for a corner suite at the hotel and wanted it to be a surprise for Liz. The room was just as he had asked for. It had beautiful marble entry, large living room area, and floor to ceiling wrap around windows. The bathroom boasted a large walk in shower with dual heads and deep whirlpool tub big enough for two. Antoinne was pleased to see the flowers and champagne he had ordered were already in the room. He lit the candles he found in the bag Liz had packed and hung their clothes in the closet before returning to the lobby to find her.

"How's the room?" She asked.

"It's fine." He answered. He wanted her to be surprised when they went up later. "Are you winning?" He asked.

"I'm up a hundred bucks!" She announced.

"Great, cash out and let's go to dinner, I'm starving."

"Me too." She answered as she hit the button to cash out her machine. With her ticket in hand they walked toward the restaurant. They dined at Wolfgang Puck Steakhouse. It was the nicest restaurant in the casino, it was a beautiful, simple setting with natural wood tables and amazing lighting. Antoinne had the filet with lobster tail and Liz ordered the petite filet with grilled mushrooms. They shared a bottle of wine, which was quickly going to her head. Over dinner they discussed their day. Liz told Antoinne about a new article she had been asked to write about a couple's resort in Jamaica. She was excited that they would hopefully be able to take this trip together. He then told her about the upcoming litigation over the property in Flint Township. Liz felt so attached to this land because it was the first property, he had ever taken her to see. It was where he had hoped to build his dream house. But before they could even get clearance to break ground, they discovered the land was protected. There was a bird that made its home on his property and it was under environmental protection laws so Antoinne was prohibited from building on his land. The litigation was with the previous owner who had been aware of this and did not disclose it when he sold him the property. Michigan law was a little grey about disclosures on vacant land. Antoinne was not the type of man who would turn around and sell the property again without disclosing this type of liability. Since the property could not be built on it was basically worthless to Antoinne or any other investor. It was frustrating and costly to go after the previous owner, but he said it was a matter of principle and he had to do it. Liz understood his feelings but wished he would just let it go, she hated to see him so stressed out. But Liz knew one thing to be true after their ten months together, Antoinne was the most stubborn man she had ever met and once he made a decision, he rarely changed his mind. Some days it infuriated her beyond words. After dinner they returned to the casino area to do a little gambling. Liz knew her time here was limited because Antoinne hated to throw away money. Jenna sent a text message that said, "Maybe next time, have fun." Liz was looking forward to seeing her best friend but didn't mind having the evening alone with Antoinne. He found a roulette table that wasn't too crowded. Liz preferred to play Let It Ride poker, but the tables were packed. Antoinne asked for two hundred single chips for her and ten twenty-dollar chips for himself. He played black and only black, Liz bet the numbers. She bet their birthdays, Jackson's birthday and a few of her favorite numbers. She put a few chips on each number. The first number to come up was a black four. They both won. The second number to come up was a black six, they both won again. In thirty minutes, they were up five hundred dollars which would cover their costs for the hotel and dinner and still leave a little extra. They decided to quit while they were ahead. They cashed in their chips and her winning ticket from earlier and proceeded to go up to their room. Antoinne lead Liz to the elevator with his hand on the small of her back. Once alone he kissed her softly on the lips and pressed the button to take them to the concierge level on one of the upper floors. He slid the magnetic key into the door and opened it for her. Liz was in awe, it far exceeded her expectations. She went toward the windows to take in the amazing view. Antoinne walked up behind her and wrapped his arms around her waist and began to kiss her neck softly. Liz leaned into his body. She felt safest in his arms. She closed her eyes and took a deep breath, she was so thankful for him. Antoinne's hand rubbed her thigh. She turned into him and wrapped her arms around his neck. His mouth met hers.

"Happy Anniversary Baby" He whispered.

"Happy Anniversary and thank you so much for a beautiful evening." Liz wondered if he would ever really know how much she appreciated him. She had an overwhelming feeling of gratitude; her life was exactly where she wanted it to be. She slipped out of his arms and walked toward the bathroom. She stopped at the closet and retrieved her lingerie. Once alone she took off her dress and her bra and slipped on her red baby doll, that matched her thong. Her large, firm breasts poked through the lace top. She left on her heels and thigh highs. Liz brushed her teeth, washed her hands and reapplied a light coat of gloss to her lips. Antoinne turned on some soft music and went to the bedroom to be sure housekeeping had turned down the bed for them. It was perfect. Liz walked in behind him as he was undressing. She watched him remove his sweater and jeans. His body was smooth and sexy, the color of dark chocolate. His muscles were defined perfection. He stood with his back to her in his boxer shorts. She approached him and kissed him gently between his shoulder blades. He retrieved the champagne and glasses and poured some for them both. "Damn Woman." He said, looking her body up and down with an eye of approval. She laughed at his response to her. "Let's toast to us, to the new house, and to an amazing future." Antoinne said raising his glass to her.

"I love you, and our life together and I couldn't be happier." Liz said. They both took a sip of their champagne. Antoinne then took her glass and set them both on the bedside table. He led her to the bed and laid her down softly. He took off his boxers and laid down next to her. He admired every inch of her with his eyes as he stroked her arms.

"You look so beautiful" he whispered while tracing her protruding nipples with his fingertip. Liz pulled his neck forward bringing his mouth to hers. He lifted her nightie half way up her stomach exposing her red thong for his admiration. He kissed her hips. Sucking and teasing her skin. She rubbed his bald head encouraging him to continue. "You are so sexy in this, but I want it off of you now." He whispered. Liz sat up as he lifted the nightie over her head and tossed it to the floor. His finger caught the corner of the panties and in seconds she was naked before him. He took her hips and rolled her body on top of his. She lowered her nipples to his mouth. Liz sucked his neck and worked her way down his body, tasting his skin, gently biting his hips, teasing his stomach until finally she took his manhood between her lips. "Oh God" he moaned.

"I prefer Goddess." She teased. They both laughed. Liz loved making him feel good. She knew she could do things to him that would make a place for her permanently in his heart. Things no other woman would ever do quite the way she did, she owned this part of him, and she knew it and loved it. He pulled her back up to him and kissed her, his tongue sending shock waves through her body. He rolled her onto her back and parted her legs with his. His fingers locked with hers as he pinned her arms to the bed. "Do you want it?" He whispered in her ear as his muscles kept her in his firm control.

"Yes" she moaned as he kissed her again and rubbed his body against hers. Liz's hips were moving in anticipation, waiting to feel him enter her. She felt his hardness taunting her. Finally, he pushed inside of her. She gasped as her body rose up off the bed responding to the shock of his thrust. His mouth met her shoulder and bit softly.

They made love to each other until the sun came up and finally their aching bodies gave way to sleep. At noon they checked out of the hotel, in search of a restaurant still serving breakfast. "What time do we need to pick up Jackson?" Antoinne asked.

"Joey's parents are taking the boys to the see the Detroit Lions play the Jets today, they said they would bring him home but I don't expect it will be before eight or nine tonight, the game starts late this afternoon and they are going out to dinner when it's over so we have the whole day free." She said with a smile. "What would you like to do?" She asked.

How about we drive over to the new house? He suggested. Liz needed to measure all the window for curtains. It was important in these neighborhoods where there were a lot of foreclosures to get the windows covered immediately, a vacant house was screaming "Rob Me!" to the neighborhood thugs. The security alarms were scheduled to be installed Monday, but they often didn't stop a determined thief. Liz and Antoinne had looked at many houses that had already been robbed of their plumbing, furnaces, water heaters, fixtures and even brick. Liz had been shocked to learn how hard some people worked at not working. A few weeks ago, Liz had unlocked a lock box to a house and as they entered, they heard voices, it turned out there were squatters residing in the vacant home, and they had interrupted a couple of crackheads getting high. Antoinne pushed Liz back out the way and pulled the door shut before she even realized what was happening. They called the listing agent as they pulled away from the property to let him know his listing was a crack house and that they wouldn't be interested in purchasing it. The agent didn't seem surprised, this was becoming epidemic in many Detroit neighborhoods. The foreclosure rate and vacant homes far exceeded anything mentioned in a newspaper report. Thieves cleaned them out of anything valuable and left the houses to rot. Broken windows and stolen plumbing meant a house filled with mold, and it was suddenly worth next to nothing. When houses were a dime a dozen no one was going to take the time to gut a house filled with mold. She often wondered who would eventually be responsible for tearing down all these uninhabited properties. Antoinne had told Liz that day that under no circumstance was she to ever go into one of these vacant homes alone, he referred to her as "A victim waiting to happen." She didn't like being told what to do but she knew he was looking out for her safety. Women like Liz weren't commonly seen here, and she drew attention wherever she went. It was a little frustrating because it would have saved them both a lot of time if she could do a quick walk through when he was at work and rule out the houses that she knew needed too much repair. After measuring the windows, he told her that he wanted her to keep the budget at ten dollars a window. She started to laugh but she knew he was serious. It was ok, she knew every nickel they kept in their pockets added to the bottom line and their profit margin, so she was up for the challenge. He took her a discount store and she was able to find curtains and rods for less than ten a window, a couple would require a little sewing, but she didn't mind. He was impressed with her ability to shop on a such a tight budget and still find something that looked nice in the house. Liz explained to him that when Jackson was little their budget was so tight, she didn't have a choice but to stretch every nickel in to a twenty-dollar bill. He respected her so much for being able to always take care of her son even when she was struggling and doing it alone, she never gave up she just did what she had to do. When Jackson was small, she took on side jobs cleaning houses just to help cover expenses, but her son never went without anything and that was the all that mattered to Liz. She would take care of him no matter what she had to do. All the lighting had been stripped by thieves so before they could even begin work, they needed a few supplies, so after curtains were bought, they went to the home improvement store. They bought light bulbs, mops, brooms, trash bags, rubber gloves and took several paint swatches with them to hold up on the walls. Liz would be in charge of the colors, he knew it would be subtle and tasteful. The work crew was starting Monday, after they finished the demolition and put up new drywall, she would be able to pick out tile, cabinets, paint and light fixtures. For now, they needed to just get the place emptied. Liz offered to go over and start cleaning but Antoinne said he would have the crew take care of that, no woman of his was going to be cleaning up someone else's grime

and dirt. "I don't mind, it will save us money if I do it." She suggested.
"Hell naw" He responded firmly. She was silently relieved not to have to do the initial cleaning. "Let's go home." Antoinne said. "I think my throat hurts." Liz drove home so he could relax. He went to bed, and she did some work on article she was writing about Disney World resorts. Liz had taken Jackson to Disney every year since he had turned four so this article would be easy, and she knew she could have it finished in a couple of days. When Antoinne finally woke up he was feeling worse. She had made some chicken soup for him and gave him a couple Ibuprofen. He went back to bed to rest. Liz waited for Jackson to get home and they played a game of Clue. It was nice to have a few hours with Jackson, he told her all about the football game and how much fun he had, she loved his animation, there was an energy young people gave off that was refreshing to be around. Jackson was thrilled to beat his mom at Clue "Better luck next time Mom." He mused. He kissed her and headed to bed.

Chapter 7 The Ugly Truth

Monday morning Antoinne was still sick. He was running a fever and felt terrible. Liz offered to make him a doctor's appointment. "Yeah, I guess I should go in, I feel like I have strep throat. "I am not sure where I put my insurance card though."
"It's ok, I can look it up online for you, it's Blue Cross right?" She asked.
"Yeah, but never mind, I can do it later. I am gonna sleep a little while longer." He responded, rolling his back to her and shutting his eyes.
Liz decided to go ahead and look up the insurance and get him an appointment with his doctor, she knew he needed an antibiotic. First, she needed to take Jackson to school and drop off her article on Disney Resorts to her agent. She took her laptop with her so she could stop and visit her grandmother when she done. She thought it would be better to let him sleep today in peace and quiet. After Liz dropped off her article she went straight to her grandmother's, where a cup of coffee was waiting on the table for her. Grandma was from the old country and her coffee was so strong a spoon could stand up straight in the cup. She hadn't seen her in a week and had missed her. She knew at some point she would have to accept the fact that her 85-year-old diabetic grandmother wouldn't be around forever, but Liz couldn't even imagine what her life would be like without her there. Her grandma loved her so much, Liz could do no wrong in her eyes. It had always been a place of refuge for her. Grandma was that one person who always took her side, even when she was wrong. Liz thought everyone needed someone who loved them completely unconditionally like her gram did. Liz plugged in her laptop and began to search for Antoinne's doctor. She was making him an appointment to see the doctor whether he liked it or not. Liz knew his family doctor was still in Flint, she did a search and quickly found their office number. She dialed the phone and told the receptionist she needed to make an appointment for her boyfriend to see Dr. Singer. The woman asked for his name and date of birth, Liz quickly rattled off Antoinne Fredericks and his date of birth. "I am sorry ma'am but the only Antoinne Fredericks we have listed has a different birthday, well actually it's the same birthday but year I show makes him three years younger than what you stated"
"No that cannot be correct" Liz replied. "Maybe I have the wrong office, I guess I will call him and call you back, thank you for your help."
"No problem just gives us a call back" the receptionist replied before hanging up.

"That's strange." Liz muttered. She knew she still had copies of their purchase agreement for the house in the car, it would have his social security number and a copy of his identification on the papers. She ran out to the car and retrieved the file "That's better." She said to herself as her grandmother cut her a piece of coffee cake. Liz pulled the file from her briefcase. For some reason his date of birth wasn't filled in, that's odd she thought.

She explained to her grandmother what the receptionist had said.

"Well honey maybe you have the wrong date and the doctor's office is right." She said simply.

"No, he's five years younger than I am, not eight." Liz replied. "I better call him, he is going to need to get this straightened out." Liz decided to do a little more internet searching before calling Antoinne and waking him up. She went to a people search engine and put her research skills to work. "He better not has been lying this whole time to me." She thought. Liz felt a knot tighten in her stomach. She was beginning to see little spots in front of her eyes as her blood pressure went up. Liz found a site that would pull up his driving record for ten dollars. She pulled out her credit card and entered the information. It said the same thing the doctor's office had said. He was eight years younger than she was, not five. Liz was not good with stress. She knew she was about to come undone. "Hell, no this fool has not been lying to me for almost a year." She said to herself. Liz was about to blow. Her temper had been known to get the best of her sometimes. She thought she finally past that and thought only Jackson's dad had the ability to push her beyond sanity. Liz grabbed her cell phone and dialed Antoinne. He didn't answer. She immediately redialed. He picked up the phone. "Hey Baby." He answered.

"Hey, are you still at home?" She asked. She was ready to head to the house and confront him face to face.

"No, I was feeling better, so I am going over to the property to meet the contractor, why what's up?" He asked.

"Well I took it upon myself to try and make you a doctor's appointment and when I called the doctor's office, they couldn't find anyone with your date of birth, the receptionist said that the only Antoinne Fredericks they have on file is three years younger than you are. I thought at first it was someone else with same name, but the birthday is identical to yours, except for the year and that is a little more than a coincidence doesn't you think?" She was pissed, and he knew it.

"Nope, I am not sure what that's about, but it isn't me." He responded, sounding guilty.

"Seriously?" She yelled into the phone.

"It isn't me." He said quietly.

"Ok, well I am at my grandma's I will call you later." She hung up the phone before he could even say "Good bye."

Liz was so angry she couldn't see straight. She had spent ten months of her life being completely honest with this man about everything. Her past, her drama with her son's father, every question he asked she answered honestly. This fool had been lying to her about his age and God knows what else! What about Jackson? Liz felt her heart drop. She knew right then this had all been some sort of game to him, that he didn't care about her or her son. He was just a lying son of a bitch. She wanted to call Jenna, but she knew she was still in class and wouldn't be able to answer the phone. She sent her a text message while driving toward home that just said "Antoinne lied, he's only twenty-nine! I'm gonna set it off!" Liz was enraged, driving way to fast toward home, although she wasn't sure what she was going to do when she got there.

Her text message beeped at her Jenna replied "Be careful Pal, don't do anything you will regret, I will call you when I leave here. Just breathe."

Liz was too angry to even think. She replayed her conversation with him a few minutes earlier. He completely denied it. He didn't realize she had already known the answer to the question before she asked it. "He thinks I am just fucking stupid!" She screamed as she hit the steering wheel so hard it bruised her hand. When Liz arrived home, she immediately plugged in her laptop to begin her search. She needed to know everything, what else was he lying about? He clearly had no problem being dishonest since he continued to lie to her face when she asked him point blank. Liz sat down in front of the computer, her hands were shaking so badly she could barely type. Tears were running down her face. "Twenty fucking nine, he's twenty-nine! No wonder he hasn't talked about marriage! He's eight years younger and not even close to being on the same page." Liz was devastated. Liz logged into yahoo. It asked for her screen name, and she typed in Antoinne's. It asked for his password and she didn't know it, so she clicked the "forgot password" tab. It took her to his security question. "What was your high school mascot?" Liz did a quick internet search and discovered the high school he went to in Flint had just changed their mascot, it was no longer the Indian's because it wasn't politically correct. Liz went back to the security question and typed in "Indians." It redirected her to his email account, she was in. "Oh God, what the hell am I doing?" She asked herself. She began to peruse his inbox. He had thousands of emails, going back a couple of years. Liz decided to only focus on emails since she had met him, what went on before her wasn't really relevant. She pulled up his history from ten months prior, there was an email dated a week after they met from a woman named Shawnie, "Well that's a pole dancer's name if I ever heard one" Liz said aloud, clicking on the email she read "Hi Baby, it was so good to see you the other night, it made me realize how much I miss you, when you make love to me I feel like I know we are meant to be together forever."

Liz jumped up out of her chair and ran to the bathroom to throw up. Tears ran down her face as she sat back down and stared at the computer. She checked his out box to see if he had responded. He hadn't. "So, he was with her after he met me?" She questioned herself. Liz's cell phone rang, it was Antoinne. She was hysterical when she answered it. "You are lying son of a bitch! She screamed into the phone. I hate you! How could you do this to me, and to Jackson? Have you ever told me the fucking truth about anything?"

"Baby, please! Calm down. I am sorry, I didn't know how to tell you. I never thought we would end up in a relationship, and when we did, I didn't know how to come clean without losing you. I swear I never meant for it to go on this long. I swear I didn't, I love you and I am sorry."

"Really and are you sorry for fucking your ex-girlfriend Shawnie after you met me?" She sobbed into the phone.

"What?" He said in an almost whispered tone.

"See once I confronted you and you lied again, I decided to find out what else you are lying about, so I am in your email right now!" Liz was hysterical. Years of being lied to by Jackson's dad were hitting her in the face. She could not believe it was all happening again.

"You are in my email account right now? What the hell are you doing? Baby, stop! Don't start doing shit you won't be able to take back. Just calm down I am on my way home right now." Antoinne tried to sound rational, this just pissed her off more.

"If you show up here right now you bastard, I swear to God I will stab you, don't you dare even think about coming here. Oh, and by the way I am emailing your ex from your account as we speak. I will read it to you. "Dear Shawnie, Antoinne and I have been together for almost a year now, in fact we started dating a week before you apparently fucked him last. If you are still fucking him, please advise and I will be happy to send his belongings to your trashy ass."

"Baby, don't send that I can explain. It was a long time ago, and you and I weren't in a committed relationship yet. I was with her a couple days before we met, I needed to be sure I was really done with her, that was it, I didn't respond, and I haven't spoken to her since then."

"See that's the thing, I can't believe a fucking liar!" Liz screamed as she hit send. "As a matter of fact, I am going to send out a mass email to everyone in your address book and ask them to please contact me if they know anything else you might be lying about."

"God damn it Liz! You need to get a grip and stop this nonsense! Don't you dare send out an email like that, the whole world doesn't need to be involved in our drama, and a lot of those people are business contacts!" Antoinne was furious now.

"Send!" She screamed. "Oh, and I changed your password, you can't access your account!" Liz put her head down on the desk and continued to sob into the phone. "I trusted you so much. I loved you so much. I wanted to spend my life with you, and it was all a fucking joke. What am I supposed to tell Jackson? I'm grown I made my choice, but what about my little boy? He loves you so much. He sees you as his father! How could you do this to us?" Liz was crying so hard he could barely understand her.

"I didn't mean for this to happen. I swear I didn't. Every night I laid next to you and I tried and find the words. I didn't want this to happen. I didn't want you to freak out. I didn't know how to fix it Liz. I'm sorry." Antoinne cried into the phone.

"Well fuck you." She said calmly and she disconnected the call. Liz crawled back into the bathroom and vomited again. She laid down on the cool bathroom floor and sobbed. Antoinne continued to hit redial on the phone until Liz finally turned it off. At two o'clock Liz sent her mom a text message and asked her to pick up Jackson from school and keep him for the night, she told her she had a meeting. Liz was grateful her mom was able to take care of her son, she was in no shape to see him right now. Liz was exhausted from the emotional outburst and finally cried herself to sleep. She woke up a few hours later to Jenna calling.

"Hey Pal." She said hoarsely into the phone.

"Are you alright?" She asked.

"No, I'm not." She said as she began to cry again.

"I broke into his email, he slept with his ex around the same time he met me. He said it was before our first date, but I don't really know. Everything is a just a fucking lie." Liz cried.

"Oh shit, does he know you were in his email?" Jenna asked.

"Yep, I have him locked out of it, and I sent out a mass email to everyone in his address book asking them what else he might have lied about." Liz said quietly.

"Oh Jesus! You didn't?" Jenna said shocked.

"I did." Liz cried harder, knowing she had made a bad situation so much worse.

"Well now what?" Jenna asked.

"Jackson is staying at my parent's house tonight. I am going to pack all of Antoinne's stuff and call him to come and get it. I would rather Jackson not be here for that part. God, I don't know what I am going to tell my son." Liz began to sob again.

"He will be fine, are you sure you want to do that? You don't think you can fix it?" Jenna asked.

"I know Antoinne and he will never get over me breaking into his email and involving other people in our mess. It's better if I just pack his stuff now."

"Do you want me to come and help and you?" Jenna asked.

"No, he put all his big stuff in storage, he can go stay in Flint, his parents still have a house there and it's empty. Antoinne goes up there once a week to check on it, it won't be a problem for him to stay there. All I need to do is pack up his clothes." Liz could feel her chest tightening.

"Ok Pal, well I am here if you need me." Jenna knew Liz was going to have so many regrets in the upcoming weeks. She would hate herself for losing control and saying horrible things to Antoinne. She would feel sick for breaking into his email and for behaving the way she had. Liz had a history of over reacting. It was rare but there was no stopping her when it happened. All Jenna could do was listen to her best friend cry over the next several months about all the mistakes she had made. Jenna knew Liz had a good heart, and Antoinne was so much different than Jackson's dad, but Liz had learned this behavior from the years of going back and forth with that asshole. She knew there was a part of Liz that would never fully recover from that relationship, and that is why Liz reacted the way she did. She compared Antoinne to Jackson's dad and she made a horrible mistake. Liz pulled a few storage bins out of the basement and began to pack his things. Tears ran down her cheeks as she held his clothes to her face taking in his scent. When everything was packed, she picked up her cell phone and dialed Antoinne. "Hello." His voice was strained, and Liz could tell he had been crying.

"Hey, I packed all of your stuff. I think it's better if you come and get it tonight while Jackson is at my parent's house." Liz began to weep.

"Ok." His voice was barely a whisper. "I'll be there in an hour; can I please have the password to my email account?" He asked.

"Oh, yeah it's *asshole*." She replied. "See you in an hour." She said and disconnected the call. An hour later Antoinne knocked at the front door. The gravity of the situation hit her when he didn't use his house key. When she opened the door, he placed the key and his garage door opener on the entry table. "I packed everything, but the bins are too heavy for me to carry, they are in the bedroom." She said quietly.

Antoinne followed Liz toward their bedroom. Liz sat down on the bed and pulled her pillow to her chest. He stood at the foot and stared at her.

"I'm sorry Liz, I really am." He said quietly.

"I don't know how I am going to explain this to Jackson." She began to cry.

"I will call him in a couple of days, I hope it's ok if I still talk to him." Antoinne's chin began to quiver.

"Of course, it is, you know that." Liz replied.

"I didn't know how to tell you the truth Liz, I swear I didn't. Every day it was like this huge weight on my shoulders. I lied in the beginning because I knew you wouldn't go out with me if you found out my real age. I wanted to see what it was like to date an older woman. I never thought it would get this far. I never thought I would fall in love with you and once that happened, I didn't know how to fix the lie. Even when you confronted me this morning, I thought I couldn't tell you something like that over the phone. I swear I was going to tell you everything tonight. I swear I was. I didn't realize that you would take it upon yourself to get the information. I certainly didn't think you would break into my email." He said angrily.

"Well when I asked for the truth and you still refused to give it to me you left me no choice."

Liz replied.

"You had a lot of choices Liz and you made all the wrong ones. When you love someone, you don't do that kind of shit." Antoinne screamed as he picked up a vase off the dresser and threw it at the wall. It shattered in a million pieces. Liz began to sob into her pillow. "That stupid fucking email you sent out went to several business associates, I am going to lose money over this!" He was getting angrier. "I need to get the hell out of here before I make a bad situation worse." He was shaking he was so upset. He carried the bins to the car. He returned to the door and looked at Liz. "Tell Jackson I will call him in a couple of days, or he can call me anytime." He said quietly. "For whatever it's worth Liz, I really loved you." Antoinne had tears running down his face as he turned and walked back to his car and left. Liz collapsed on the floor and sobbed. Finally, she cleaned up the mess of the shattered vase. After moving the furniture and making sure there were no remnants of glass, she made a cup of tea and took a pillow and blanket to the couch, she knew there was no way she could lay in the bed they shared. She sat awake all night reliving the events of the day. Already she wished she could go back and undo what she had done. She wished she would have stayed calm and talked to Antoinne in person instead she knew she threw the match on the fire and burned any chance they may have had at reconciliation. At one in the morning her phone rang. Liz was still awake. It was Antoinne he was drunk and crying. "I loved you so much. I can't believe you just threw all that away. It's gonna take me a minute but I will get over you." He cried into the phone.

"Where are you?" She asked.

"I'm hanging out with my boys, they are taking care of me." He responded.

"You aren't driving, are you?" Liz questioned.

"Nah, I am way too drunk to drive. God Liz how could you do this? How could you call me all those names and break into my email? I lied because I didn't want to hurt you and today you did everything you could to destroy me." He was crying. Liz began to sob.

"I felt like you were just using me when I found out you were lying, and then I asked you and you still lied. I am sorry." She knew she was going to vomit again.

"Yeah me too." He said and he hung up the phone. Liz ran to the bathroom and threw up again. "God, please I am begging you, please fix this for me." Liz prayed. Liz knew with every fiber of her being even God wanted no part of the mess she had made. The next morning Liz picked Jackson up at her parents to drive him to school. He could tell when he got into the car she had been crying.

"What's wrong? Why have you been crying?" He asked.

"Well, Honey, last night Antoinne and I broke up." She replied quietly.

"Why?" He demanded. "What did you do?" Jackson was on the verge of tears as he screamed at his mother. "You ruin everything! I am gonna go live with him and you can just be by yourself!" He screamed.

"Jackson, calm down. You and Antoinne will still be friends. He cares about you very much. He said he will call you in a couple of days or you can call him anytime you want to." Liz said trying not to cry.

"I hate you. First you chase my dad away and now you did the same thing to Antoinne." Tears rolled down Jackson's cheeks and he continued to scream at his mother. Liz put her head down on the steering wheel and cried. "Just take me to school!" He yelled.

Liz didn't say anything else. She drove him to the school in silence. He got out of the truck and slammed the door in her face. Liz knew it would be a long time before her son forgave her. He loved Antoinne like a father and he was going to feel this loss as deeply as she did.

Chapter 8

The first few weeks were hell. Liz couldn't get use to sleeping alone again. She tossed and turned and hugged her pillow. She had never been so depressed in her life she was pretty sure she was gaining weight by the hour. She had always been an emotional eater and she had gained eight pounds in the three weeks since he left. Her conversations with Antoinne had been strained at best. He was still in regular contact with Jackson. Liz was so grateful to him for that. She knew he could turn his back on her son if he chose and it would have devastating effects on him. Instead he continued to call and text Jackson. They emailed every couple of days and made plans to spend time together over the weekend. Antoinne had told Jackson he would take him go kart racing if it was ok with his mother. Liz of course agreed. He showed up at the house to get Jackson. She hadn't seen him since he moved out three weeks earlier. They had talked about the house and the progress that was being made by the construction crew, but they didn't discuss their relationship. She was in her room working on an article when he walked in. "Hi" he said.
"Hi, how are you?" She asked politely.
"I'm ok, Jackson and I were gonna take off. I am gonna take him go kart racing and maybe to the batting cage if that's ok with you?" He said.
"Yeah, it's great, thank you, he's having a tough time. I made sure he has plenty of cash on him so today is my treat." She didn't want Antoinne to have to spend his money entertaining her son.
"I think I can handle the cost of go karts." He said in an annoyed tone.
"Oh, I know, I just didn't want to put any sort of burden on you." She replied, feeling uneasy. She hadn't meant to offend him.
"If it was a burden, I wouldn't do it Liz." He answered as he turned his back to her and walked out of the room.
"That went well." She said to herself. A few hours later Antoinne brought Jackson home. Liz was disappointed he didn't come inside. "Did he just drop you off?" Liz asked Jackson.
"Yeah." Jackson had already made it clear his loyalties lied with Antoinne and not his mother.
"I hope you remembered to thank him." Liz added walking away.
"I'm not a baby mom, I think I can handle saying thank you." He replied in a nasty tone. He had become almost impossible to live with since the breakup. Liz knew he blamed her because Antoinne was gone. He was hurting too, and she was the closest one for him to lash out at, so he did. Liz tried to just ignore it, she felt like it was all her fault too. Liz walked to her room and grabbed her cell phone. She sent a text message to Antoinne. "Thank you, he loves you so much." Antoinne didn't respond to her. She knew he was angry. Liz was riding an emotional roller coaster. Part of her was sorry for breaking into his email, and another part of her was so furious at him she wanted to slap his face, but more than anything she wished she could go back in time and do it differently. She wished he had been honest, and that they didn't have this huge wall between them now. Liz knew they had to find a way to salvage some sort of friendship, for her son's sake and for their business relationship. They still owned a house together and it was months from completion. It was yet another cause of tension between them. She had found this house to flip and it had turned into a money pit. It

needed far more work put into it than either of them had anticipated. She knew he was blaming her for the talking him into buying it. At this point he was probably blaming her for global warming and world hunger too. Liz wished he would beg her forgiveness. She wanted him to come back groveling and crying. She wanted him to say she was the best thing that ever happened to him and that he would buy her the biggest engagement ring in the world if she would just forgive him and agree to be his wife. She let out a heavy sigh. It would never happen, Antoinne was stubborn and had too much pride to do any such thing. Liz knew it, but she couldn't give up hope. She was constantly fantasizing about him being back home with her and Jackson, she was still buying groceries for three, picking up his favorite things in case he showed up. She left his dresser drawers empty. She felt like her life was on hold until he came back. Liz began to resent him for not trying harder to fix their relationship. It was an emotional roller coaster ride. Every day it took every ounce of energy she could find to put one foot in front of the other and just go on. She had a child to take care of and Liz knew that she could never ever put him through anything like this again. Her soulmate was gone, and it was her fault and now she must live out her punishment, a life sentence alone. Liz had never brought men into Jackson's life for a reason, and now everything she feared had come to fruition. Her son was grieving as much as she was, and he had done nothing to deserve it. Everyone had told Liz that being a single parent was hard, but she truly had no idea when she got pregnant that it has turned out this way. She knew in her heart that even though she loved Jackson's dad it was unhealthy and toxic relationship that had chemistry and nothing else. It was three years of one-night stands and he certainly never loved her, in fact she doubted he was capable of really loving anyone. She was ready for a baby and he was smart and handsome, and she knew their child would be perfect, but looking back it was so selfish. She didn't think that it would be so hard. She didn't think that her child would walk around for his entire life with an open wound from not having a decent father in his life and that he would never see it wasn't his fault and if he did then the only person to blame was her. How could one person be so stupid? How was Liz going to live with so much regret? How could she fix this for her son? She lost the love of her life and he was never coming back so how does she learn to accept the consequences of her actions and move on alone forever? Liz knew after what she did to Antoinne he would never trust her again. He was young and beautiful and smart, he would move on quickly, Liz would never recover. God was punishing her for all of her selfishness and arrogance, she had burned her last bridge and there was no way to go back and she had no idea how to go forward.

Chapter 9

It had been four weeks since Liz had seen our spoken to Antoinne, they had communicated about the house via text messaging. His conversations with Jackson had dwindled and pretty much stopped as she knew they would. It was too painful for everyone, but she was angry. How dare this man lie to her for so long? Why didn't he just tell her the truth? Why did she lose complete control and destroy everything so they could never fix it? So many times, in her life Liz had loved men who were unworthy and couldn't be trusted but she really believed he was different and when she discovered he lied she lost her mind. Why? Did she really think she was so unworthy of love that she had to completely destroy it every time it came close? The worst part was it couldn't just be his fault! She topped his wrong doing and did one better so now she couldn't just be mad at him, she had to be filled with sorrow and regret for her own part in destroying what was the happiest she had ever been. It would so much easier if she had left him groveling for her forgiveness and taken the high road but instead, she crawled into the gutter and started slinging mud and shit like common trash. Now she had to face him. He had asked her to meet him at the house to sign some papers and do a walk through with the contractor to finish it up and get it on the market. This would be the end of the road, once they sold the house there was nothing left tying them together and he would be gone forever. A few short weeks and there would be no excuse to text or to reach out, she felt a panic rise in her throat and took a deep breath to steady herself. Time to shower and look her absolute best before going to meet him. Today was critical, she wanted to make him miss her so much. She wanted to make him beg to be close to her just once more. Liz was careful in every selection this morning. His favorite shampoo and perfume. She had a perfect new dress, a black wrap dress that came just above the knee and had cute ruffle along its edges to make it flirty, the plunging neckline was the kill shot. She put on her earrings and a long necklace to rest in her cleavage. Her makeup was light, not too heavy, she didn't want him to see how hard she was trying, a soft, pink gloss made her lips completely kissable. She blew out her hair and flipped up the ends, so it was soft and natural hanging down her back. Her black, lace panties and bra would give it away but if he got that far then her plan at seducing him would have worked and there was no point in pretending innocence. She threw on black heeled boots, thank goodness her legs were still tanned and probably her best feature, she needs everything in her arsenal if this was going to work.

Liz pulled up to the house, Antoinne and the contractor were standing in the driveway talking. She put her sunglasses on her head and made sure her dress was up high enough to show a respectable amount of thigh when she swung them out of the car. Both men watched her intently as Liz moved with confidence from her SUV. Her smile was big, and she was undaunted, this man would never know she felt like she was bleeding to death because of him. Liz had too much pride to let him see she was broken into a million pieces. Today she would leave him wanting her and missing her so much that he wouldn't be able to think straight. She approached the two men reaching her hand out to the contractor, "Good Morning gentlemen" she leaned into Antoinne planting a fast kiss on his cheek, making sure he was able to catch a whiff of her perfume. He looked stunned by the gesture, but Liz kept moving and talking as if it were nothing, not allowing him time to process anything for too long. "I am so excited to see the progress you have made on the house so show me everything!" Liz said in her most animated voice, taking command of the situation. The contractor unlocked the door, as Liz walked up the steps Antoinne instinctively put his hand on her back to steady her on the old porch, but quickly withdrew when he realized what he had done. Liz felt her heart flutter at his touch and break a little when he pulled it away.

The old brick house was charming. The rooms were large and open with ten-foot ceilings. The trim was all six inches and each room had carved crown molding. The giant staircase had been refinished to its original grandeur and gave the feeling of elegance. They didn't build houses like this anymore, had it been in the suburbs it would easily sell for half a million. Liz stared into the marble fireplace and for a fleeting moment pictured her and Antoinne making love on a beautiful rug in front of a roaring fire. She pushed the thought from her head and moved on to the kitchen. No one wanted a house with an old kitchen and these homes proved especially challenging because the kitchens tended to be small and lacked adequate space for storage. Liz had talked Antoinne into knocking out the breakfast nook and expanding the kitchen. This is where they had spent a large chunk of the budget.

The kitchen was magnificent, they had been able to salvage the original wide plank wood floors and added white shaker cabinets with leaded glass doors and solid surface white countertops. Liz wanted marble but Antoinne was right when he said this neighborhood was ok, but it wasn't going to get a price that warranted marble. Still it was the nicest house on the block, and she knew they would have multiple offers as soon as it went on the market, if they didn't it would be one more thing for him to blame Liz for, after all the twenty-five-thousand-dollar kitchen upgrade was her idea, not his. Liz needed this house to be a money maker, maybe it would help him forgive her if she helped him make a lot of cash. She knew logically that money had nothing to do with their issues but hoped he would see her as more of an asset than a huge mistake if he had a nice return on investment. They all continued upstairs, the stained-glass window on the landing had been repaired and was reflecting beautiful prisms of color down the hallway, it was a perfect touch to remind buyers of the history and charm this old house had to offer. Antoinne walked passed Liz and said "I have a little surprise to show you" he opened the bathroom door to show Liz a beautiful antique claw foot tub. "I thought about what you said, and I think you were right when you said kitchens and bathrooms sell houses, so I had the old tub restored and put in the new flooring you picked out, what do you think?"

Liz was stunned. She knew this was never going to be their home, but he was still considering her opinion and trying to make her happy, that had to mean something right? Was this just a gesture of goodwill or a strategy to make money or was it an olive branch meant to help repair their broken relationship? So many thoughts were racing through her head. She took a deep breath and ran her finger along the marble vanity. "It's perfect" She whispered.

The contractor broke down the costs for them, they made a list of the last few items that needed completing. Liz would call for staging, Antoinne would call a landscape crew, the contractor was taking care of the touch up paint, within a week they would have a for sale sign in the yard.

The contractor said goodbye and left Liz and Antoinne standing alone in the living room. "So, are you happy? With the house I mean? She added quickly, not wanting to talk about the state of their nonexistent relationship.

"We are sixteen thousand dollars over budget, so I am stressed, I will be glad when we get it sold." He replied in an agitated voice.

" Well I am confident we will get multiple offers the day it hits the market" Liz tried to sound like she was sure of herself even though secretly she was terrified they may not make a profit and Antoinne would have one more reason to blame her for ruining his life.

His eyes locked eyes with hers and Liz felt overwhelmed with emotion, it was taking every ounce of self-control she had not to throw herself at him and sob into his chest. She reached out touching her fingers to his. He squeezed her hand and pushed it away.

"Don't" he said firmly. Liz felt tears begin to fill her eyes. She willed them back, she did not want him to see her cry, but it was too late, they betrayed her and spilled onto her cheeks. She felt her hands begin to tremble and crossed her arms to keep him from seeing her begin to melt down.

"I guess I should go" she walked toward the living room to collect her purse and keys from the fireplace mantle. Antoinne approached her from behind and wrapped his arms around her. Liz felt like she was going to collapse. So many emotions flooded to the surface, she leaned back into him and let the tears run down her face. God, she had missed the safety of his strong arms around her. She turned into him and his mouth met hers. He kissed her urgently. His hands grabbing at her like he was starving, and she were his last meal. Liz loved that he wanted her so badly. She knew it meant that he wasn't over her. Suddenly he stopped, he pushed her back.

"No, damn it, no, we aren't doing this!" He was so angry that his body was fighting him, and he was battling every instinct he had to take her. "I can't go back. It's too much! I can never trust you again!" Liz knew that she should walk away and leave but she needed to be close to him, she needed their bodies to heal what their hearts could not. She looked him in the eyes and without saying a word she untied her wrap dress, letting it fall open, exposing her perfectly chosen black, lace bra and panties. "Please don't" he whispered. She took a step closer and let the dress fall off her shoulders. "This won't fix anything Liz, you need to stop" She walked closer and put her hand on his neck pulling him into her, she kissed his mouth. "Liz please, I am begging you to stop." His words and his body were still in disagreement and Liz opted to follow the lead of his body. She reached for his belt, feeling his manhood hard against his jeans, she let out a soft moan. Antoinne finally gave into his primal urge he grabbed Liz by her waist and kissed her hard. He ripped her bra and panties from her body, he was hungry for her, but he was too angry to make love to her and Liz could tell everything was different. The gentle soul who was always careful to protect her and keep her safe was not the man before her now. He roughly grabbed her breasts as he bit her neck. She put her hands on his chest to slow him down and gently pushed him back. He grabbed her wrists hard. "This is what you want, Liz right?" Liz did want him, even this side of him. "Yes" she whispered. He backed her against the wall hard and lifted her onto him, he thrust himself hard and fast inside of her. Liz couldn't breathe. He pounded inside of her while he ravaged her neck and chest with his mouth. Liz held onto to his shoulders and took her punishment with a mixture of passion and sadness. This man was not making love to her. He was taking her because he could, because she still belonged to him because she needed to know that he would not be controlled by any woman. He hammered into her over and over again. Liz hoped with every thrust he was releasing his hurt and that their bodies were healing together. Harder and harder he fucked her, she gasped and cried out. She hoped the gift of her body was something he could take comfort in, she prayed the closeness they once shared would heal their wounds. He finally exploded deep inside of her. Liz didn't realize tears were rolling down his face. He stood her up and turned his back to her. "I need to go" he whispered.

Liz was a little shocked to hear him say he was leaving so quickly, she threw her bra and panties in her purse. "Ok" she said softly, putting her dress on her sweaty body as fast as she could. He said nothing, he waited for her to step outside before setting the alarm as he turned from her to lock the door, she wrapped her arms around him and kissed his back. "Have a good day" she said softly. Liz walked quickly to her car and pulled away before Antoinne could see her start to cry.

Chapter 10

A full week had passed without a word from Antoinne. Liz's plan had failed. She had hoped the closeness they shared would lead to a reconciliation, or at the very least an admission that they shared something special, something worth saving. She was angry at herself for thinking about him so much. She didn't know how to let go. She wondered how many months or

years would pass like this, with her still missing him and wanting him. Was this her life now? She hadn't slept through the night in what felt like forever. Jackson seemed to have moved on, but she knew this could never happen again. He was still five years from graduating high school, so at least five years would pass until she had a man in her bed again. Wow, that was disheartening. The house she and Antoinne had flipped was going up on the market in just a couple days, she had talked to the contractor and emailed Antoinne a copy of the listing agreement. He signed it and sent it back with a simple "Thanks" at the bottom. Liz was meeting the stagers at the house at nine the next morning and then she would put the sign in the yard. She did not mention this to him in the email, she really couldn't see him right now, so it was best to just get in and do her job and get out. The sooner this sale was completed the faster they could all move on with their lives. Liz was resolved in letting go. Now she had a job to do, she would sell this house for top dollar and he at least couldn't say she made him lose money. The next time he saw Liz she would cold as ice and completely professional. Never again would she let him have her. Oh, make no mistake, she would look her best and tease him mercilessly, but hell would freeze over before she ever repeated what happened the week before. How dare he not cave to her feminine wiles, this man thought he could just fuck her and not beg her to take him back? So, what if she threw herself at him? So, what if he told her that it wouldn't fix anything? Clearly, he didn't know who she was, she was going to make him want her if it was the last thing she did. The next morning Liz put on her sexiest jeans and plunging bright red top with red heels that were way too high to be comfortable but just in case Antoinne showed up she needed to look her best. She had her hair curly and natural, with big, gold hoop earrings, red lips and red nails. She at least felt confident walking into the house. The stagers showed up right on time and everything was going smoothly. The house looked amazing filled with furniture. Liz was putting dishes in the built cabinets when Antoinne showed up. "Hey, the place looks amazing Liz." He remarked. She instantly noticed how he called her by her first name. No "Baby or Sweetheart" Liz knew it was deliberate, he did not want to be too familiar, he was keeping every distance he knew how to keep. Liz was not about to let him know she was still hurting over him and his rejection was not going to get to her today, at least not while he was watching.
"Well thank you Sir" she said with a quick glance in his direction. She did not make eye contact and she didn't linger, Liz tried to seem busier than she was, he was not getting her attention today. "I need to head upstairs and make the beds if you care to help" she said as she began to walk away, not sure if he would follow or not. He did. "I can make the beds how about you put the towels on the bar in the bathroom? "
" I can make a bed Liz, I will help you and it will go a lot faster" Liz strutted away toward the stairs trying to stay far enough in front of him that he would not get the feeling that she was flirting or trying to get him to notice her in any way, it was working great until she fell off her incredibly high heels down three stairs and right into his arms. He caught her nicely.
"Baby be careful! Why would you wear come fuck me shoes to set up a house anyway?"
Liz felt her face go flush. Did he really just call her out on the obvious truth?
She pushed away from him and sat down to remove the ridiculous shoes, hurling them passed his head and down the stairs. In her bare feet Liz stomped toward the first bedroom to make the bed. Antoinne smirked as he followed behind "You are like a spoiled little girl who really needs a spanking." He remarked half laughing.
"Well you won't ever touch my ass again, so it won't be you who gets to spank me" Liz said in her bitchiest tone. She pulled the sheets and pillows out of the bags in the first room. She

tossed the pillows and cases at him and began to put the fitted sheet on the full-size mattress, this room was perfect for a little girl with pale yellow walls and wide white trim. Liz brought a sweet little cloth doll to put on the appliqued quilt and a small butterfly lamp for the side table. She always wished that Jackson would have a little sister but soon she would be too old, and that vision seemed to grow dimmer every day, now she had wasted another year of eggs on a man who was too young to realize what a precious commodity her eggs were! Liz felt herself getting madder by the minute. She didn't even look at Antoinne. She quickly made the bed and moved on to the next room, he followed behind without a word. Again, she tossed the pillows at him, a little harder than she had planned, and she hit him in the face. "Oh sorry" she said casually with a smirk. He looked stunned. She turned her back to him so he couldn't see her stifling a laugh. Suddenly she felt him pull her shoulder backward and onto the bed. Before she knew what was happening Antoinne was on top of her kissing her. She tried to push him away, but he grabbed her arms and held her down as he kissed her hard. Liz couldn't believe what he was doing! How dare this man just throw her down and kiss her like they were still together! For all he knew she had a new man in her life! This arrogant jerk had some nerve! But his kiss felt so good, she was weakening, and she knew it. She was kissing him back. Why was she kissing him back?! "No, no, no" she told herself, but it was too late, her body was betraying her. She was not about to have a repeat of last week, this man would not just take her and then go on with his day like she was nobody! Liz found every ounce of strength she could muster and pushed him off of her. "Not gonna happen, Antoinne!" She yelled and stormed out of the room leaving him frustrated and flustered. "Make the damn bed!" she yelled as she walked out of the room.

Liz ran down the stairs, picked up her shoes and her bag and charged out of the house barefoot. She squealed out of the driveway as fast as her tires would carry her. She had to escape quickly before she did something she would regret. She deserved better and she was not about to become a series of quickies for this man or any other, she had been there. If Antoinne Fredericks wanted to be in her bed, then he would have to fix this mess between them, or they would both have to figure out how to live life without each other. Liz's phone rang as she barreled down 8 Mile road toward the suburbs. Antoinne's name flashed across her screen.

"What?" she fired into the receiver instead of 'Hello"

"Baby, please slow down, think about Jackson, you don't want to get into an accident."

Liz felt tears burn her cheeks. "What do you care?" She asked him, choking back sobs.

"I do care, Liz, I care too much, and I don't know what to do about it, but I damn sure don't want you getting into a car accident so please pull over for a minute, please for me." Liz knew he was right.

"Ok, I am pulling into a McDonald's parking lot. I wish they sold alcohol here, I will sit here for five minutes, I am fine, can you just finish making the beds and putting the towels out in the bathrooms? I will come by tomorrow with the sign, I am going to do an open house on Sunday."

"Not by yourself you're not!"

"Antoinne you gave up the right to tell me what to do! I am grown and we need to have an open house so I will take care of it by myself!"

"Damn its Liz! Do what I tell you!" Liz turned off her phone. Now she was going to have the open house on Sunday simply because he told her not to. Liz pulled into the drive through for a cup of coffee, and drove toward home, she was going to get her article written on the area cider mills and then she was going to email Jackson, he had been gone at summer camp with his cousin for three days and she was really missing her boy. Liz began thinking about how in a few short years he would be gone, and she would be alone. Who was she if she wasn't Jackson's mom? Of course, she would still be his mother when he went off to college and moved out of her house but like most women her identity was tied to be a mom. She wasn't a wife so her social circle was different than most. She didn't hang out with married couples. Her identity was that of a single mom, very little socializing, a lot of hard work and a lot of time spent caring for her child. She would not go back and change it; her son gave her life meaning but who would she be when she did not have him to take care of anymore? Liz thought about how much things would change over the next few years. It brought tears to her eyes to think about how lonely she knew her life would be when her son left, and she was all by herself. She was a caregiver and a nurturer, how on earth did she only end up with one child, now she was too old to start again and she sat there wishing she had three more children at home to raise and something else to focus on besides this man who had broken her heart and still thought he could tell her what to do even though he clearly did not love her anymore. Now she had to finish her article, market her open house for Sunday to all the Detroit area agents, pick up signs and balloons and figure out a way to tell her editor that the article she is scheduled to write on the couples resort in Jamaica next month can't happen because she is no longer a part of a couple and therefore she can't exactly fulfill her obligation. Liz and Antoinne were supposed to be taking the week-long vacation to the Couples San Souci resort in just three weeks and although she had hoped things would turn around for them before they were scheduled to go it was becoming pretty clear to Liz that it was hopeless and it was time to cancel, she knew she would have to pay back her publisher for their costs of the trip, it was only right. Afterall, it was not their fault that she was no longer part of a couple. She hated to have to cancel but she and Antoinne could not even be in a room together without fighting, there was no way she could convince him to go through with this vacation they had been planning together. Besides she had too much pride to even bring it up to him.

Liz would never beg any man to go anywhere with her, she never had, and she never would. It was time to focus on what had to be done and not think about how she felt. Liz knew she was strong, and she had survived having her heart broken before. She survived giving birth without Jackson's father even coming to the hospital. She survived raising a child all by herself for twelve years now without anyone to help when he was sick or hurt or just driving her crazy. She worked, she traveled, she took care of a home and she never missed a single football game her son played, she was superwoman God damn it and she was not going to be taken down by this man or any other. Liz went home and sent out a mass email flyer to all the Detroit area agents showcasing her open house for Sunday from noon until three. She needed to be home by four because Jackson was coming home from summer camp at five and she wanted to make his favorite dinner. Liz printed out twenty-five flyers highlighting the beautiful details of the house. Twenty-five walkthroughs for an open house was extremely optimistic but Liz had to feel hopeful about something. She then sent an email to her magazine publisher telling her they needed to talk about the trip to Jamaica and to please give her a call when she had a minute. This would be a difficult conversation to have, she knew Angela would ask a million questions about her break up with Antoinne and Liz just was not ready to answer them. Liz and Angela were certainly friends as well as coworkers, but it was still too raw and Liz certainly was not going to tell her publisher the sick details of her failed relationship, especially when the truth made her look so bad. She knew she needed to tell Antoinne about the open house, even if he did not like the idea it needed to be done and she was perfectly capable of sitting at the house for a few hours on a Sunday afternoon. Liz pulled out her phone and sent him a text message. "I don't want to fight but I thought you should know I am doing an open house on Sunday afternoon from noon until three, I already sent out a mass email, hopefully we will get multiple offers! Have a good day." A few minutes later her phone beeped. Antoinne responded with "Whatever Liz." She was stunned. Now they were reduced to rudeness. Liz thought it was better not to engage and decided to just leave it alone. She opened her computer and finished up her article on the area cider mills before she began researching resorts in Jamaica, maybe she could still write an article, just using a different kind of resort and a lot of internet research. She hated leaving Angela in a bind and this little mishap was going to hit her wallet hard. The trip was costing the firm over five thousand dollars and it was going to pretty much drain Liz's nest egg, which left her feeling a bit sick to her stomach. She hoped to make it back on the sale of the house, she hated feeling strapped for cash, it reminded her of those early years when Jackson was little, and she only owned two pairs of pants for herself and not many more shirts. The one thing she had learned in those early years was that she could make it through anything as long as she had her son. She also learned that being smart did not necessarily pay the bills and that pride did not feed the baby so she cleaned offices and houses and did whatever she could to make money. They had nothing extra those first few years, but they had enough to survive and that inner strength got Liz through tougher times than this one. At that point she could not have even imagined having five thousand dollars in the bank so really it was a blessing to be able to pay for this trip that she would never get to take and a reminder of what not to do in the future. Sure, if she thought about all the great places, she could take Jackson with five thousand dollars she could get really upset right now but Liz refused to get sucked down any further. She would simply cut her losses and let the healing begin. The next step in the process was to get this house sold, hopefully make a little money and then she would find a way to recover emotionally and financially. Now that she an Antoinne would not be doing any more real estate deals she was going to have to tighten up her finances anyway. It seemed like this break up was affecting her on every level, she had let this man into her life, her home, her son's life, they were intertwined financially, and all this happened in less than a year. How could she have been so irresponsible? Liz thought of a million reasons as to why she would never date again.

Chapter 11

On Sunday Morning Liz got up early to make Jackson's favorite dinner before doing her open house. He loved her homemade alfredo sauce with grilled shrimp over pasta. Liz prepped and marinated the shrimp and decided to make the sauce so she could just reheat it when she got home. She pulled the garlic bread out of the freezer and double checked that she had enough supplies for the world's biggest ice cream sundae for dessert. She could not wait to hug her baby, he had been gone for a week and she was ready to have him home! With everything ready for her boy, Liz showered and dressed, she wore a black pencil skirt, stopping just above the knee and a nice black pump, a bright green blouse with a deep v, professional but still sexy, she thought there was a good chance Antoinne would show up to see that everything was fine so she needed to look good but she was not trying too hard to get his attention. Liz arrived at the house and set the open house sign with balloons in the front yard. She put the flyers and offer packets on the entry table. The stagers had done an excellent job setting up, it looked like a beautiful house anyone would be proud to call home. Liz hoped the expected thunderstorms held out for a few hours, nothing ruined an open house faster than bad weather, people were not going to show up if it started to storm. She flipped on all the lights and lit a few candles and turned on some soft jazz everything was perfect for prospective buyers. After an hour a young couple with a new baby and their agent came to the door. Liz welcomed them, offered them a bottle of water, which they graciously accepted and gave them a tour of the home. Her love of the house was obvious as she gushed over every detail to the young couple. They too loved the clawfoot tub and extra detail in the main bathroom, it made Liz's heart skip a beat when she thought about Antoinne spending the extra money to make is special because it was important to her even though she knew it probably was not the best use of their money. He was the one who paid for the renovations and this house had far exceeded the budget, she was hoping and praying they would make a nice profit and soon. The young couple took the flyer and the promised to discuss it and be in touch, Liz had a good feeling they may be writing an offer, there was nothing in this neighborhood that had been updated as nicely as this house. Ten minutes after they left a family of seven came barreling in the front door without an agent and speaking very little English, Liz was thankful her very rudimentary Spanish was at least enough to communicate with the husband, his English was about as good as her Spanish, but they seemed to be able to get the basics understood. The children ran through the house like wild animals, and the grandmother kept yelling at them in Spanish to calm down, or at least that is what Liz hoped she was saying. An experienced agent knows you never host an open house without a purse full of candy for just such an emergency. Candy seems to be word that is understood by children everywhere. Liz lead the little beasts through the kitchen and out the backdoor to the porch and made them all sit quietly to receive the treats. She gave the oldest child the whole bag and thank goodness his English was good enough to understand that he was in charge of his siblings until she was done showing his parents and grandma around the house. The candy did the trick and she was able to give the adults the full tour. They seemed very interested in the property and since they did not have an agent it would save her the commission if she was able to write the offer herself. The husband said they had already been pre-approved, but they had just started looking, Liz told them she would be happy to show them other homes as well, so even if they did not buy this property it looked like she had a new client. It would be challenging if they wanted to take all the kids to see every house but that is why they invented candy and Liz could handle it. She gave them her contact information and set up a meeting for the following Tuesday to sign a buyer's agent agreement.

The sky grew dark and there was a loud crack of thunder. Liz jumped, she hated storms. Just thirty more minutes and she was leaving. She was surprised Antoinne had not shown up, but it was probably for the best, their encounters had been emotionally draining for both of them and the more often she saw him the harder it was to try and move forward without him. Every time he walked in the room, she wanted to wrap her arms around him and bury her head in his chest and just stay there forever. Lightning flashed across the room, the sky opened up and the rain began to pour down. The thunder cracked again, and the power went out. Liz decided to put out the candles and leave, there was no way she was going to see any more potential buyers in this weather and being in this house during a storm with no electricity was making her nervous. Just as she turned to put out the candles on the mantle, she heard the door open, she turned expecting to see Antoinne standing there soaking wet but instead there was another man, all alone and dripping from the rain. "Hi, come on in, it looks like it's getting pretty nasty out there, I was just getting ready to close up, but you are welcome to take a look around." He was about five foot ten and stocky with a full beard and large, dark eyes.

"Yeah ok, show me around" he said. Liz thought he seemed a little off and could smell the alcohol on his breath when he approached her, his jeans were dirty and his t shirt had a small hole in the neck line, his baseball hat was on backward and his eyes were bloodshot. Liz glanced at the large snake tattoo on his left forearm. He certainly didn't look like a potential buyer and she was really wishing she had listened to Antoinne and not done this today by herself.

"Are you married, or just looking for yourself?" She asked trying to get a little more information, maybe he was just trying to get out of the storm. She attempted to convince herself that the storm was making her tense, he had done nothing wrong he just came in to see the house or to get out of the rain.

"Just me." he moved in closer to her, he smelled like sweat, smoke and alcohol. It had clearly been days since he had showered.

"Well go ahead and take a look around, sorry the power is out but you should still be able to see everything ok" Liz was not about to walk through the house with this man. The hair on her arms stood up when he looked her up and down, she worried she was in trouble. Liz stepped away trying to put as much space between them as possible. With the power, out she knew the alarm wouldn't work and honestly all it did was irritate the neighbors, the police did not respond to security alarms in the city, they had their hands full as it was but maybe if it was working the noise would at least send him running. Unfortunately, that was not an option. Her instincts were telling her to run but logically he had not really done anything wrong, maybe she was overreacting, storms always put her on edge. She tried to calm herself, she took a deep breath and spoke nervously.

"The house has three bedrooms and two bathrooms, one here on the main level and one upstairs. The basement is not finished but it easily could be, it has the plumbing necessary to add another bath, which is very unusual for house this age. The bedrooms are all a nice size and the master has a beautiful sitting area." He didn't seem to be listening to anything she said. Liz walked toward the kitchen, her plan was to go out the backdoor and get the hell out of there. She did not care if she was overreacting, she needed to get out of this house and away from this man. He walked closely behind her as she went toward the kitchen. "As you can see the kitchen has been completely updated and has a wonderful butler's pantry original to the house, it offers a ton of extra storage space." He glanced over his shoulder toward the area she was pointing to and Liz took it as her opportunity to head out the backdoor. As she reached for the knob the dirty stranger grabbed her wrist. "Don't you touch me!" Liz screamed. He pushed Liz against the wall by her shoulders, pinning her hard. Liz felt dizzy as her head hit the door frame. Suddenly his hand was around her throat as he moved his face right up to hers.

"Shut your mouth bitch" he grunted at her and slapped her face hard. Liz struggled to breathe. She saw Jackson's face flash into her mind. She was not going to let this sonofabitch kill her, at least not without a fight. Liz kicked and thrashed with all her might. She lifted her knee hard, catching him perfectly where it would hurt the most. This caused him to loosen the grip on her neck and Liz was able to wiggle away from him and run toward the front door. He was right behind her, with everything in her Liz lunged for the door pulling it open but he grabbed her by her hair, her head snapped back as he yanked her inside. Liz cried out and desperately tried to escape his grip. He balled up his fist and struck her hard on the side of her face. Everything began to spin, blood was running down her cheek, her vision was blurry, and she collapsed on the floor, hitting the coffee table on her way down. With every ounce of strength, she could find Liz fought swinging her arms and legs wildly and screaming as loud as she could. Nothing could stop her angry attacker. He punched her in the stomach, Liz felt the vomit rise in her throat as he wrestled to pin her under him. Liz scratched at his face and tried to gouge his eye. He screamed and hit her again, her mouth filled with blood. He ripped her blouse open. Liz silently prayed. "Please God. please." Her attacker was on top of her grabbing her body and pulling at her skirt. Liz cried out and tried to scramble away but he overpowered her. With all her strength Liz freed her hand and dug her nails into his face. He backhanded her so hard she heard the crack of her nose as more blood gushed out of her face. Liz begged for her life. Begged him to stop as she felt his hands ripping her skirt away.

Suddenly he was off of her. Liz's blurry vision tried to make out what was happening. A foot had come flying at them and kicked him off of her. She saw her attacker trying to scramble to his feet as fists flew at his face again and again. It was Antoinne and he was going to kill this man. Liz was able to crawl out of the way, but she couldn't speak or stand. She heard the grunting and yelling as Antoinne continued to beat this man, hitting him over and over in his face. The neighbor heard the commotion and came running through the front door, he yelled for his wife to call the police and proceeded to help Antoinne pin the attacker to the ground and convinced him not to kill the man. Once the neighbor had his gun securely on her attacker Antoinne dropped to floor next to Liz. She was dizzy and she couldn't really speak. Tears were running down his face. "I should have been here, I am so sorry Baby. Just hang on an ambulance is on the way." Liz was able to whisper Jackson's name and Antoinne promised her he would take care of everything. He took her phone and called Liz's sister immediately. He promised her he would go to the hospital with Liz and she would go get Jackson. She felt his hand on hers as she shut her eyes.

Chapter 12

When Liz opened her eyes, she was not quite sure where she was or what was happening. Antoinne was sitting next to her, holding her hand and he looked like he had not slept in a week. She tried to speak but it hurt to move, and her mouth was dry. Antoinne put a straw to her lips so she could take a sip of water. He began to speak. "Thank God you opened your eyes. Do you know where you are?" Liz shook her head and whispered "No", but the word did not seem to come out.

"You are in the hospital, you were attacked at the house yesterday." Tears filled his eyes as he said the words to her. Fragments of the assault began to flood Liz's mind. She attempted to speak, her first thought was her son. "Jackson?" she tried to whisper, but again the words did not escape her throat. Antoinne seemed to know what she was going to say. "Jackson is ok, he is with your parents, your sister just left here a few minutes ago, she will be back in a little while. He only knows you had an accident and that you will be ok, we all thought it was best to just leave it at that for now." Liz squeezed his hand, she was grateful to know her son was ok. She reached up to touch her face. It was hot and throbbing. She felt bandages, she knew she must look horrible and did not want Jackson to see her this way. She felt too tired and her thoughts did not seem to be making any sense, her head was pounding, and every inch of her body hurt, she needed to shut her eyes.

When Liz awoke again her sister Caroline and her best friend Jenna were standing next to her bed talking. Her sister had clearly been crying. She gave Liz a gentle hug, it hurt so much to be touched. She seemed to know exactly what Liz was thinking. "Jackson is doing great, he is at football practice and staying with mom and dad. He is worried about you, but I have told him you just need your rest and that you will call him as soon as you feel up to it. Liz needed to hear his voice and she needed to reassure him that she was ok. Jenna brought the water to Liz and she was able to hold the cup and drink through the straw. She could not remember ever feeling so thirsty. She took several sips before she tried speaking.

"Antoinne?" she whispered.

"We sent him home an hour ago, he has been sitting by your bed for two days and he needed to get some sleep and a shower, I told him I would stay here with you tonight and he will be back tomorrow, he is really struggling and blaming himself for the attack." Jenna said. Liz felt awful, he had saved her life! She only had herself to blame, he had told her repeatedly not to be at the house alone and in her attempt to prove that she could handle herself she almost lost her life and left her son an orphan. She felt terrible that all of the people she loved were now suffering because of her stupid decisions. After a few more sips of water Liz was able to clear her throat and speak. Her voice was scratchy, and it hurt to talk. "I need to call Jackson" she said hoarsely.

"I will text mom and make sure they call you when he gets done with practice" Caroline began to text their mother while she continued to talk.

"I need to see a mirror." Jenna and Caroline looked at each other and Liz knew by their expressions that she looked really bad.

"Maybe you should wait." Caroline suggested. Liz slowly sat up, determined to get out of the hospital bed and go to the bathroom to see how bad she looked. "Don't try and stand up!" Jenna commanded, "You are hooked to IV's and the monitors behind you!" Liz asked them to get the nurse, she was not going to lay in this bed one second longer. Her sister hit the call light and when the nurse came in, she was happy to see Liz was sitting up and able to talk. The nurse assisted in getting Liz on her feet, she felt like she had been run over by a truck. Every inch of her throbbed in protest. She gently eased out of the bed, she felt dizzy as she tried to stand. Slowly, with the help of the nurse she shuffled her way to the bathroom. The nurse turned on the light. Liz gasped when she saw her reflection in the mirror. Her left eye was completely swollen shut. Her cheek had a two-inch gash that was stitched up. Her neck was a giant, purple bruise, her lip was swollen, and her nose was covered with tape holding it back it places from where it had been broken. Liz started to cry. She looked so awful. There was no way she could let her son see her like this, he would be permanently scarred. It hurt to breathe. The nurse began to speak as Liz stared at her reflection. "Ok, so the doctor will be in shortly but here is a quick run-down. Your nose is broken, three of your ribs are cracked and you have stitches on your face and on the back of your head that total over 100. There is no internal organ damage, but you do have a pretty bad concussion. And you are lucky to be alive." Liz didn't know what to say. Lucky was not exactly the word that was crossing her mind right now.

"I really want to take a shower' she said softly.

"No problem, I believe your sister, or your husband brought a bag of your things if you would like I can help you get cleaned up and get into your own nightgown and robe."

"Thank you" Liz tried to stop crying. Right now, she just needed a hot shower and to process everything that she had just been told. She did not correct the nurse about Antoinne being her husband, she was not sure what he had told them and did not want to do anything that might jeopardize him being able to visit as often as he could. Liz stood under the steaming hot shower and sobbed. She cried because she physically hurt, because she looked so terrible that the sight of her would traumatize her son, because Antoinne could have been hurt or killed trying to rescue her. She cried because this bastard took away a piece of her that she would never get back, she would never feel safe again, he stole that from her. She would be vulnerable the rest of her life. She cried because she would forever be looking over her shoulder. She cried because everyone she loved had to stop their lives to help hold hers together. She needed to talk to her son. She needed him to know that she was ok and that she would be home as soon as she could. After her shower Liz felt a little better but just that small task exhausted her. She put her head back on her pillow and shut her eyes. Jenna and Caroline had gone to get a cup of coffee and she needed to just rest for a minute. An hour later Liz woke up to the ringing of her cell phone. Caroline must have set it next to her knowing Jackson would be calling. Liz saw his name flash across her screen and cleared her throat to try and sound her very best. "Hi Sweetheart! How are you?"

"Mom? Are you ok?" He sounded so worried, it broke her heart.

"Yes baby, I am a little banged up, but I will be fine! I will hopefully be home soon. Are you doing ok at grandma's?"

"Yes, I am fine. I just miss you and I want to come and see you" He sounded like he might cry.

"Well I am pretty banged up, it looks a lot worse than it feels but I don't think you would like to see me like this sweetheart."

"I just need to see you Mom! No one is telling me anything! Please!"

"Ok, honey don't get upset. I will talk to grandma and have her drive you up tomorrow ok? How about tomorrow morning? She asked in her calmest voice.

"Yeah I have to go to school and get my classes and my locker, so maybe she can bring me after I finish." Jackson sounded relieved.

"Ok, then get a good night sleep and I will see you tomorrow. I miss you so much, I can't wait to see you."

"I miss you too mom, I love you."

"I love you too baby. Goodnight."

Liz hung up the phone and hoped her sister had packed some makeup in her bag so she could try and cover these bruises a little before her son came in. She still did not know what she would tell him about what had happened to her. Liz was laying there feeling sorry for herself when Antoinne walked through the door. Tears instantly hit her cheeks. He looked ten years older. He was drained and exhausted. He had a bruise under his eye, clearly a remnant of his heroics when saving her life. He walked to her bedside and leaned in to gently kiss her on her forehead. "I am so sorry" Liz sobbed. "Look at your eye! You look exhausted, I am so, so sorry! This is all my fault, I should have listened to you!" Liz couldn't catch her breath. Her cracked ribs made crying hurt so bad. Antoinne stroked her face. Tears ran down his cheeks. "Shhh. It's ok, stop crying Baby. It's ok. All that matters are that you are ok. I thought I was going to lose you. I have never been so scared in my life. I should have never let that happen to you." He could barely talk, Antoinne was trying desperately not to cry, he was emotionally drained.

"No, you saved my life! I can never thank you for what you did for me, if you had not shown up when you did that bastard would have killed me and my son would not have a mother!" Liz cried. She had so many regrets. She wanted desperately to hug him, but she hurt so badly.

"Please?" Liz patted the bed and motioned for Antoinne to sit next to her so she could hug him. Antoinne laid next to her and Liz put her head gently on his chest and cried until she could not cry anymore. He cautiously stroked her hair. He wanted to hold her tight, but he was careful not to squeeze her, he was so afraid he would hurt her. He saw just how fragile she was. Her beautiful face was beaten and bruised. Her whole body was hurting, and he laid there wishing he had killed the sonofabitch who did this to her. He was so angry and so scared. Had he just got there sooner none of this would have happened. When Liz finally stopped crying, she told him about her conversation with Jackson and how upset he was. Antoinne knew why she agreed to let him come see her, he knew Liz needed to see him and hold him as much as he needed to see his mama. He told Liz he would be there when Jackson came and maybe after their visit, he would take him to get some lunch and pick up whatever he still needed for school, classes would be starting in a week. Liz appreciated him so much. She knew Jackson would love to spend some time with Antoinne and it would be a good distraction after her sees how bad she looks. Liz closed her eyes, she felt so safe on his chest, listening to his heartbeat was all the medicine she needed she thought as she drifted off to sleep.

When Liz woke up it was early morning and Antoinne was gone. There was a young, tall doctor with very short dark hair and green eyes standing next to her discussing her pain medication with the nurse. "Good morning, how are you feeling today?"

"I am not sure yet" Liz replied trying to sit up and gather herself. She hated how exhausted she felt. Moving even slightly seemed to require all her strength and hurt every inch of her body.

"Well the good news is that you are on the road to recovery, your vitals look good and I think we will be able to send you home in a few days assuming you will have some help when you get there."

"Oh, she will have plenty of help, I will be there to take care of her." Antoinne responded to the doctor as he walked in the door carrying a beautiful bouquet of wildflowers.

"Well I would like to schedule a couple weeks of physical therapy when you get out here to help you get your strength back. I would also like to set you up with a psychologist who helps people deal with this kind of trauma and I am going to prescribe an anti-anxiety medication. I would like you to have it on hand just in case. You have been through quite an ordeal and it's going to take time for you to heal physically and emotionally." The doctor said matter of factly.

Liz had not really thought too much about this yet. Right now, it was so hard to just move physically she had not thought about the damage done to her spirit and her soul. She nodded her head in agreement as the realization that she might not ever be the same again began to register.

After the doctor left Antoinne helped Liz get up so she could shower and get ready for Jackson to see her. "I don't want him to know what happened to me" Liz told him. "I think it will scare him and make him really angry."

"I agree but you need to be careful that you don't lie to him either, maybe just leave out the details and tell him when you feel better you will talk more about it. Maybe it is something you can ask that psychologist about when you go in." Antoinne suggested.

"Yeah maybe" Liz looked down. She suddenly felt embarrassed and ashamed. Antoinne was seeing her at her absolute worst and they both realized that she was probably not going to be ok for a very long time. "I am so sorry Antoinne" Liz felt the tears coming again.

"Hey now, it's ok, and Jackson is going to be here any minute so let's not cry ok?" Antoinne was right, Liz did not want her son to see her upset.

She wiped her eyes and tried to think of something pleasant. "Thank you for the beautiful flowers." She smiled through her swollen lips. Antoinne helped her to the shower so she could look her best before Jackson arrived and then went to find her real coffee, she desperately needed a hot cup of caffeine and the hospital was not serving anything close to what she was used to. Jackson arrived just after eleven with Liz's mom. Her mother instantly teared up, but Liz gave her look, letting her know she needed to pull it together in front of her son. Jackson ran to her bedside and froze as he reached out to hug her. "I don't want to hurt you!" He was so upset.

"It's ok sweetie, just hug me gently" Liz pulled him into her arms. She had never been more thankful than she was at this very moment. "Hey, the doctor said it looks a lot worse than it is so I should be able to come home in a couple days, but I might need you to help me out a bit when I do ok?"

"Yeah mom, I will do everything, and you can just rest!" Jackson replied.

"I love you, my sweet boy, this will all be over with soon, I promise." Liz told her son as she stroked his cheek. Jackson was telling his mom all about football and how he was starting Wide Receiver for the season opener this weekend when Antoinne came back in.

"Antoinne!" Jackson exclaimed jumping up to give him a hug. "Guess what I get to start at Wide Receiver on Saturday, it's our first game!"

"That's great buddy!" Antoinne was genuinely excited for Jackson. "Hey how about we go over to the sports store and get you knew cleats for your game, your mom told me that yours are too small, and we can pick up whatever else you need for school?"

"That would be awesome!" Jackson could not contain his excitement.

Liz just smiled at the two loves of her life, Antoinne was such a good man. The distraction kept Jackson from asking any questions about how his mother ended up in the hospital which was a big relief. Right now, Liz just wanted his life to be as normal as possible. Antoinne told Liz's mom he would drop Jackson off in time for practice that evening and the two of them headed off to spend the afternoon together. Liz's mom was drilling her with questions about the attack, Liz pretended to be fuzzy on the details, telling her mother she did not really remember most of it, there was no point in putting either of them through the horrific details, it required more strength than Liz had and since no good could come from it she knew there was really no point in upsetting her mother. When she finally left the physical therapist came in to show Liz how to move properly until her ribs healed and how to take extra precautions when dressing and showering since she may feel off balance for some time to come. Liz was ready to go home and sleep in her own bed so she was thrilled when the doctor told her she would be discharging the next day. She immediately texted Antoinne. "Good news, I get to go home tomorrow morning!" She typed. He responded immediately "Great, I will pick you up and I plan on staying with you until you have made a full recovery." Liz thought she should tell him it was not necessary, that he had already done too much for her, but she couldn't. She just typed back "Thank you" and left it at that, she said a silent prayer thanking God for keeping her alive and Antoinne and Jackson and the people she loved. Now more than ever she knew she needed to count her blessings and not focus on her pain or her disfigured face or she would spiral into a deep depression and she owed her son her best self, even if that self was not recognizable in the moment.

Chapter 13

The first few weeks at home were brutal for Liz. She could barely stay awake. When she was awake every loud noise made her jump, she was scared of her own shadow. She knew it was ridiculous and that logically she was perfectly safe, but she was terrified whenever she was alone. Even though Antoinne was there taking care of Jackson she felt depressed and anxious, which made her angry because she was determined in her mind that she would not allow this attack to define her or change her, but it had. She stayed in her room most of the time. She woke up from nightmares several times a night. Thank God Antoinne was there, she knew she would be lost without him. Liz hated feeling this way. She despised that this monster had stolen her spirit and left her physically and emotionally ruined. Her body was healing but her face still showed traces a yellow and purple bruise. Antoinne was so angry over the attack, he was on edge and calling the prosecutor every few days for an update to be sure the piece of garbage who attacked her was going to suffer as much as possible. She hated that he blamed himself and that he was so angry. Liz was intelligent woman, she understood that men and women processed trauma very differently and that he needed to work through it in his own way but when he hit the punching bag in her basement (that he said was for Jackson but Liz knew better) for hours every night she jumped out of her skin and tried to cover her head with her pillow to block out the noise. Liz did her best to put on a good face for him because the worse she seemed the angrier he became. She had gone to a couple counseling sessions and she knew more than anything she just needed time, they both did. Antoinne slept with his arms wrapped around her every night. He needed her to feel safe. Neither of them had even mentioned the status of their relationship or if they even had one. He kissed her gently and rubbed her back but that is where the physical contact stopped. Antoinne was terrified he would hurt her every time he touched her. Liz knew if they were going to be physically intimate then she would be the one to initiate it, and she felt scared, but she needed to be close to him again on every level.

She decided it was time to get out of the house and try and get her life back. She told Antoinne that since she could now cover her left-over bruises with makeup she wanted to go to Jackson's game on Saturday. It was going to be a perfect Michigan fall day with temperatures in the sixties and the sun would be shining. It was exactly what Liz needed and maybe they could go to the cider mill after the game, she craved some normalcy. He seemed happy that she wanted to leave the house. She was excited to watch Jackson play, he had a starting position and had scored a touchdown at the first two games that she had missed. When Saturday arrived, the weather was perfect just as predicted. It was going to be about sixty degrees and sunny. The leaves were in the highlight of their color change. It was Liz's favorite time of year. Antoinne made sure to bring a bleacher seat and pillow for Liz, he was worried it would hurt her to sit for so long, but she was feeling much better and even if she was a bit sore, she was ready to face the world again and she was tired of hiding out. Jackson immediately spotted his mom when he took the field and gave her a big wave. It was exactly what her heart needed. The game was filled with excitement, Jackson ran the ball for a fifty-five-yard touchdown in the first quarter and turned and pointed to his mom when he scored. Her and Antoinne were both beaming with pride and laughing at his cockiness. He scored two more times and his team won the game by six. They left the field and went and picked up cider and doughnuts from the apple orchard. Liz let Jackson invite one of his friends from the team to come along. The boys had a great time retelling the highlights of the game and each and every play to Antoinne and Liz as they drove. Their excitement was contagious. After the game Liz agreed that Jackson's friend could sleep over. Antoinne said he would grill burgers for the boys, and they all seemed happy with that plan. Liz was exhausted, she had a great day but now she needed a hot bath and a cup of tea. Antoinne and the boys turned on television to watch the Michigan State Spartans play a night game while Liz snuck off for bubble bath. She texted Antoinne from the tub and asked him if he would bring her a cup of tea. When he came into the bathroom Liz thought about how the intimacy between them had changed. She would never again worry about him seeing her without her makeup on, or her hair not done. This man had seen her battered and beaten covered in blood. He took care of her and he helped her shower and he loved her at her very worst. They shared something now that could not be removed from either of their hearts, it brought a stronger sense of familiarity and a bond that could not be broken. Liz knew that their relationship problems were not fixed but she did not worry about them the way she had a month ago, he was here with her through the worst time of her life and he was not going anywhere. She loved him so deeply she could not imagine her world without him. "How about you undress and get in this tub with me?" She smiled up at him.

"I would love to, but I promised the boys I would be right back, and I don't want them to come looking for me." Antoinne replied as he reached down to and kissed her lips softly.

"Ok well wake me up when you come to bed ok?" Liz asked.

"Are you sure?" Antoinne questioned.

"Yes, I am sure." Liz shaved her legs and underarms, she put on some lightly scented coconut oil and dressed in only lace panties and a tank top. She knew she could not stay awake until the game ended so she hoped Antoinne would wake her up when he came to bed, she shut her eyes and drifted off to sleep.

When Liz woke up the sun was shining, and she could smell coffee brewing. Antoinne had not woke her up when he came to bed. Her chest felt heavy with disappointment, she got up and brushed her teeth and threw on a pair of sweats and t-shirt before making her way toward the kitchen. "Hey good morning sleepyhead!" Antoinne said as he handed Liz a cup of coffee.

"Thank you, good morning." Liz wasn't going to make a big deal about him not waking her up, maybe he was only here until she was healed up and then he was going back to his life and he did not want her after all. "Where are the boys?" Liz asked. They just finished breakfast and I told them I would take them to the park and throw the ball around for a bit, is that ok?"

"Yeah, you guys have fun, I am going to get showered and try and do some work, if I don't start making some money we are going to be in serious trouble!" Liz said only half kidding.

"I paid all your bills for you this month. So, you don't need to worry about anything. Oh, and we have a full price offer on the house, I showed it to a young couple a few days ago and they called me this morning and the sent over the offer!"

"Wow, that is great news!" Liz was happy the house was sold, she never wanted to go there again. "Thank you for taking care of the bills, I will pay you back, just let me know what I owe you." Liz didn't want him to feel like he was obligated to take care of her financial problems when she wasn't even sure what the status of their relationship was. Besides she was an independent woman!

"No, you won't, stop now. Just say thank you and move on to a new subject" Antoinne replied firmly.

She knew when he had that stubborn tone if she continued it was going to turn into a fight. "Well thank you. Thank you for everything you do for us, I couldn't possibly ever express how grateful I am to you." Liz told him as she moved toward him and wrapped her arms around his neck.

He hugged her gently and lightly kissed her neck.

"Damn, woman! I have to take these boys to the park! Don't start that right now!" He teased.

"Ok, you go! I am going to go get showered." Liz winked at him and moved away before Jackson or his friend walked into the kitchen. After she showered and dressed, she sat down at her computer and began going through her emails. She had purposely been avoiding contact with the outside world as she just did not want to talk about what had happened to her, she did not need to talk about it or relive it again and again, she just pulled herself into her safe little nest with Antoinne and Jackson and she felt no need to include anyone else right now. Liz knew people were simply concerned and wanted to help but they kept asking if she was ok and what had happened and she did not want to tell people that she was not ok, and she would never want to talk about the attack, every time she thought about it she tried to push it out of her head. She also could not stand the pitiful stares she was getting, she just wanted life to be normal again. Liz opened an email from her agent Angela who had been incredibly patient during this whole ordeal. She told Liz she had been able to reschedule the Jamaica trip, Liz had never been able to tell her she did not think she would be able to go and now she wondered if she should even bring it up to Antoinne. She was so happy that he was there, but she still was not sure if it was out of guilt, obligation, love or all three. She decided it was time to put him to the test.

Chapter 14

Tuesday morning Liz went to see her agent with two freelance articles on vacationing in northern Michigan. She grew up spending her summers on the northwest shores of Lake Michigan in the small resort community of Charlevoix so writing about a place so near and dear to her heart, along with the neighboring city of Petoskey was easy work. The articles practically wrote themselves. Angela was in the office hacking away at an article on her desk with a red pen when she walked in. She jumped up to hug Liz when she saw her come in. It hurt a little, her ribs were still a bit sore, but she was thankful for the welcomed greeting. The receptionist brought both women coffee and they spent the next hour talking. Angela asked Liz how she was feeling and what was happening with the prosecution. Much to Antoinne's dismay Liz begged the court advocate to have the prosecutor offer a deal to her attacker, the last thing Liz wanted to do was go through a lengthy trial reliving every horrific detail over and over again. Antoinne said he understood but he wanted to make sure the scumbag who attacked her was locked up for a very long time. It was a touchy subject for them to discuss. He tried very hard to be patient and understanding but he was so angry he did not want a deal offered. He also did not want Liz to have to spend days in a courtroom with this piece of garbage, he knew how hard it would be for her, so he was trying to do what was best for her but what he really wanted was for this guy to be locked up forever. The prosecutor assured them both that he would go for attempted murder charges if the attacker who she learned was named James did not take the deal they were offering which was his only chance of being out of jail in the next ten years. The prosecutor assured them that since he was a repeat offender the judge would hopefully give him the maximum penalty. She was praying he would take the deal because she felt sick to her stomach at the idea of having to sit in a courtroom with him or worse get on the stand and tell a room full of people every detail of what happened to her. She knew she did nothing wrong logically, but she still felt ashamed and embarrassed. According to her therapist that was a normal reaction, but it did not feel normal to Liz. Yes, she was angry and scared, and she understood those feelings, but it made her ever madder to feel ashamed that she was attacked. She filled Angela in on the details of the case and how amazing Antoinne was being. Angela told her she would like Liz to pick a date for the following month to go to the Couples San Souci resort in Jamaica. Liz knew she needed to bring the trip up to Antoinne, but he had already done so much for her she was not sure how she could ask him for one more thing.

After her meeting with Angela, Liz met up with Jenna for lunch. It was a parent teacher conference day and Jenna did not have any meetings set up until after two, so they had a couple hours to grab a bite to eat and catch up.

"Hey Pal! It's been forever!"

"Hey, you're right, how are you?" Liz asked as the waitress showed them to their booth.

"Just ready for this day to be over, these conferences are student lead, so I have to sit there and listen to these kids tell their parents complete lies about how they are doing in school and then I get to break into the conversation and shock them with the truth about their little beast of a child. Good times."

"Yeah, sounds fun! So what else is new? How are things with MaryBeth?" Liz asked. Since her attack she really had not been much of friend to anyone, it felt nice to hear about someone else's life for a change and not be so focused on her own issues.

"Terrible actually, I think it's time to move out." Jenna replied rather casually.

"What? Why haven't you called me? What is going on?" Liz said surprised and upset that she had no idea her best friend's personal life was falling apart.

"Well it's not like you haven't had a lot going on! I didn't want to add to it by dumping my problems on you." Jenna replied.

"Sorry, I haven't been much of a friend the last couple months, tell me what is going on right now." Liz demanded.

"Yeah you suck, and for no good reason" Jenna said sarcastically, shaking her head at Liz. "She is crazy and moody, she does nothing around the house, she fights with me every time I ask her to help with the bills, like I make enough on my teacher's salary to support to her! I hate going home, it is really tense and awful, and I have been looking for an apartment."

"Wow I had no idea! What can I do to help?" Liz asked.

"Nothing just watch for the fire, I have a feeling when I tell her I am leaving she is going to burn down the house!"

"Well keep the hose close by and call me if you need me to show up with an extinguisher!" Liz said jokingly.

They got caught up over lunch and made plans for Jenna to come out Saturday to Jackson's game. He would be thrilled. On her way home Liz stopped at the grocery store and picked up steaks, potatoes, the makings for a good salad, garlic bread, Antoinne's favorite apple pie and some vanilla ice cream. He had been doing all the cooking and taking such good care of them that she wanted to make him a nice dinner and just show him a little appreciation. Once arriving back at the house Liz decided a good cleaning was first on her list of things to do. The men in her life had done their best but it was not to her usual standard. She would never complain but it felt good to scrub her sinks and tubs and wash her floors, but not on her hands and knees, her body was still too weak so today a mop would have to do. It was good therapy for her, and she loved the results, Liz always liked to clean to clear her head, it helped her sort out her feelings. She lit the candles and turned on some soft music before she showered and slipped into a light blue cashmere blended lounging pants and matching top. It was soft and comfortable but still feminine enough to be sexy. Liz was going to make her move tonight to get her relationship back to what it should be. Yes, she and Antoinne had grown closer than Liz could have ever imagined over the past six weeks but that had not reconnected sexually yet. She knew Antoinne was scared he would hurt her, and he was treating her like a fragile flower. She appreciated his love and tenderness, but she needed him to be with her completely and totally and she needed to feel him again. She might not be swinging from any chandeliers for a while yet but that did not mean that she couldn't make love to her man. She just was not convinced that he wanted her. She knew he loved her, but she was not positive if he was there out of guilt and obligation or because he wanted her back. Tonight, would be the night she got the answers to this question.

When Antoinne and Jackson finally came in after practice Liz was on the back deck grilling the steaks. Jackson gave her a big, sweaty hug he was happy to see his mom acting like her old self.

"Hey mom! Those steaks look great, I am starving!"

"Well hit the shower Babe and dinner will be on the table when you get out." She hugged him again, pointed him toward the shower and turned her attention to Antoinne. "So how was your day, Handsome?" She asked as she moved in to kiss him.

"It was good, I got the closing date for the house, it's going to be this Friday afternoon. If you don't want to come you can just have your signature notarized and I can go, it's up to you." He said as he leaned down and kissed her again.

"I want to be there." It's not like we are doing it at the house, it's fine. Do the buyers know?"

"Yes, I would not feel right selling anyone the house without telling them, besides the couple both are Detroit police officers so they would have found out anyway and they are both armed and dangerous, they are not worried about their safety." Antoinne told Liz.

"Good, as long as they know." Liz said softly, eager to change the subject. "So, are you hungry?" she asked, moving toward the fridge to get them drinks.

"Starving!" He exclaimed.

"Beer?" She asked reaching in the fridge for two of them.

"Sure, sounds good." She grabbed a water for Jackson set the drinks down on the table and went back to pull the steaks off the grill before they were overcooked. Dinner was perfect. Jackson told them both all about his day at school and practice. He was excited for the game on Saturday, it was their homecoming game and it was against the cross-town rival team. He was again starting at wide receiver and was very excited, he had proven himself to be one of the best on the team. Liz let them talk game strategy while she cleaned up the kitchen. After dessert was served Jackson could barely keep his eyes open. He hugged them both and

headed off to bed. Liz knew he would be sound asleep in five minutes. She snuck down the hall and into his room and sat on the edge of his bed and stroked his hair. He was just dozing off and opened his eyes for a brief second. Liz kissed him on his forehead. She missed her baby. Jackson was taller than her now and certainly not a baby. She wanted to crawl in next to him and read him a story and sing "You are my Sunshine" to her little boy just one more time. Where had the time gone? She wondered as she felt her heart break just a little. She snuck back out of the room, pulling his door shut tightly and joined Antoinne on the couch where he was flipping channels. "Is he ok?" Antoinne asked.
"Oh, he is already asleep, I just need to sneak in one more kiss, he is growing up too fast" Liz snuggled into Antoinne, he wrapped his arm around her and rubbed her back lightly while they watched tv. She kissed his neck softly and slid her hand under his shirt. Liz rubbed his chest, slowly working her hand to his belt she unfastened it quickly and undid his button on his jeans. Antoinne put his head back and shut his eyes as she stroked his growing erection. Liz moved off of the couch and onto her knees between his legs. She releases him from his jeans and took him softly between her lips. He let out a deep moan and wrapped his hand in Liz's hair. He watched her intently as she took him deeper and deeper into her mouth and throat. She loved making him feel good. It had been months since they made love and as much as she was enjoying making him feel good, she wanted him inside of her. Liz pulled back slightly, teasing him with her tongue, she was not going to let this end too soon she thought. She pulled his jeans off all the way and stood to drop her pants and panties on the ground. Antoinne reached for her waist, bringing her down on top of him. "Oh God" he moaned. Gently and steadily he glided his body inside of hers. Their mouths and bodies intertwined perfectly. "God, I love you so much" she whispered in his ear. He kissed her hard. She had not realized how much she had missed being close to him. Loving him and letting him love her. It was different now, they shared a new level of intimacy, forged in pain but solid and without pretense.
"I love you more" he groaned as moved faster and harder until he exploded deep inside of her. Liz collapsed on top of his sweaty body. She knew if she didn't get him up and to bed right away there was a very good chance, they would fall asleep right there on the couch. She kissed him softly and stood pulling him to his feet. Quietly they gathered their clothes and walked hand in hand to bed where Liz closed her eyes with her ear to Antoinne's heart and his arm around her.

Chapter 15

Over breakfast the next morning Liz knew it was time to bring up the trip to Jamaica. If he hesitated at all she would later tell him it was cancelled. The last thing she wanted was him going on a romantic holiday if he was not interested in a long-term relationship again. Liz made coffee for herself and began to scramble eggs and fry bacon for Jackson and Antoinne, she cut up some fresh pineapple and strawberries and popped wheat bread in the toaster. Normally she saved big breakfasts for the weekend, but Jackson needed the extra calories, he had definitely lost a few pounds, between football and him growing at a rapid rate Liz worried he would get too skinny, not a fear she ever had for herself. "Good morning" Antoinne whispered in her ear as kissed Liz on the back of the neck while she poured the orange juice.
"How did you sleep?" Liz asked.

"Like a baby! You put it on me good!" He laughed.

"Shh! Jackson might hear you!" Liz laughed and pushed him gently toward the table.

"He is still in the bathroom, he can't hear us." Antoinne replied.

"Great, then before he comes out, I was hoping to ask you a question. Please don't feel like you have to answer right away and please don't feel like you have to say yes. It's just that you have done so much for me already and this would be something nice for both of us, but it might be too much too soon for you, so I don't really know if I should even bring it up." Liz rattled on nervously.

"Baby, just spit it out." Antoinne, smiled as he took his vitamins and swallowed a big gulp of orange juice.

"Well Angela said she was able to reschedule the trip to the Couples resort in Jamaica and I obviously can't go there alone, I mean even the name Couples Resort says it for Christ sake. I don't know why she would schedule it without asking me first and I can probably just tell her it's not a good time, I'm sure after everything that has happened, I think she will understand if I tell her I can't do it right now. Plus, what about Jackson? I don't know what I was thinking, he doesn't need me gone right now. Just forget it, I don't know what she was thinking, it's a terrible idea. I should have never brought it up." Liz felt like she might cry.

"Are you done?" Antoinne asked very calmly.

"Yes, I am sorry, you have already done way too much for me, let's just forget it." Liz all of sudden felt very guilty for even mentioning this to Antoinne. He has gone so far above and beyond for her and now she was asking for more. She wished she could go back five minutes and take it all back. Damn Angela anyway, she thought.

"Ok, because if you are done, I was going to say that I think we could both really use a few days away and I would love to go with you to Jamaica. I can't take two weeks off or anything but if we could do five nights, I could certainly make that work, what do you think? He looked at her with complete love and Liz couldn't help but cry.

"I think that is perfect, I don't want to leave Jackson for longer than that and I would love nothing more than a few days alone with you on a beach in paradise." Liz threw her arms around his neck and kissed him over and over.

"Hey! Gross! No kissing in the kitchen, people eat here!" Jackson protested loudly as he entered the room.

"Good morning Sunshine. Sit down and eat or you are going to be late." Liz walked over and purposely kissed his face.

"So, what are you so happy about?" Jackson asked, as he plopped down at the table and began to eat like he had not been fed in a month.

"Well, actually that is something I need to talk to you about. I am supposed to go to Jamaica to write an article about a couple's resort and Antoinne is going with me. Kids are not allowed at this resort, so I was going to see about you staying at Aunt Caroline's for a few days. What do you think?" Liz worried that after everything she had been through in the last couple months, he may be nervous having her go away.

"Great mom has fun! Bring me back something cool. We gotta go, if I am late, I will get detention." Jackson replied without a single bit of concern.

"C'mon Buddy, I will drop you on my way to work." Antoinne said as they both quickly shoveled a couple more bites of food in their mouths. Liz grabbed their lunches out of the fridge, kissed them both and sent them on their way. She cleaned up the breakfast mess, made herself another cup of coffee and went to her office area in her bedroom to email

Angela and to ask her to please keep the trip to five days and try and schedule it for a few weeks out, she wanted to wait until football, and hurricane season ended at the end of October, so hopefully she could get them set up for the first or second week of November. Then she researched the resort a bit and the surrounding area for her article. Liz knew if they were only going to be there five days it was important that she narrowed down the highlights and planned out the best way to make the most of their time without packing in too much. She was finishing up when her phone rang. Liz's heart dropped when she saw the caller ID "Wayne County Prosecutor." She thought about letting it go to voicemail and decided she better just get it over with or they would probably just call Antoinne. "Hello" Liz said cautiously.

"Ms. Bartlett this is Joseph Sullivan, I am one of the prosecuting attorney's for Wayne County, I hope I didn't catch you at a bad time?"

"No Mr. Sullivan it's fine, what can I do for you? She asked.

"I am calling to tell that James Simmons has decided he wants to go to trial and he is not taking the plea." Liz dropped the phone. She fumbled on the desk and picked it up quickly.

"Ms. Bartlett are you still there?" he asked.

"Yes, I am here. Why is he doing this?" Liz asked.

"He is a repeat offender and has nothing but time on his hands in jail and since it's not costing him anything, he is going to drag this out and hope for a sympathetic juror. To be honest Ms. Bartlett, I am not surprised at all, but I am sorry you are going to have to go through a trial."

"I am not sure I am willing to do that Mr. Sullivan." Liz said angrily into the phone.

"I understand how you are feeling right now, but unfortunately subpoenas are in process for you and Antoinne Fredericks, we owe it to every woman out there to lock this piece of garbage up for a long time." Mr. Sullivan stated very matter of factly.

"Mr. Sullivan, don't you dare assume you know how I am feeling unless you can tell me you have been attacked and almost raped like I was. Has that ever happened to you sir?" Liz was furious.

"No ma'am, I did not mean to imply that you" Liz cut him off before he could finish.

"I am ending this conversation now, I need time to process this before I say anything else. When are you expecting this trial to start?" She asked angrily.

"Two weeks Ms. Bartlett, probably the first week of November. It should last three or four days." His tone had changed to a much gentler one.

"Thank you for the information Mr. Sullivan." Liz stated firmly and hung up the phone. Her hands were shaking, and she felt like she might vomit. She crawled back into her bed and pulled the covers up tight over her and began to sob into her pillow. She did not want to go through any of this, she did not have the strength to relive the worst thing that had ever happened to her and she could not sit in the same room with the piece of shit who did this to her. Her phone rang again. Liz saw it was Antoinne. She wiped her face and cleared her throat, she did not want him to know she was crying. "Hi Babe." She said softly, there was no hiding her tone from him, he knew her too well to be fooled.

"Hey, Mr. Sullivan just called me, you ok?" She could hear the concern in his voice.

"No, but what can I do?" She started to cry.

"I am coming home." He sounded upset.

"No! I am not going to have you running home to take care me like I am completely unstable, I will be ok. I promise." Liz wanted him there next to her making everything better, but she knew she needed to toughen up and deal with this. "I am going to go to the mall for a couple hours and look for some end of summer clearance sales, maybe I can find a couple new sundresses for our trip. We can still go right?" Liz asked.

"Yes, Baby, of course we are still going. But I can come home if you need me to, seriously I don't mind." She could hear the concern in his voice.

"I know, and it's one of the reasons I love you so much but really it's ok. I am a little shook up, but I know you will be right there by my side and we will get through it. I am angry now and that sonofabitch is not going to intimidate me ever again. I need to call Angela and have her schedule the trip for the second or third week in November when this is all done." Liz felt a surge of anger shoot through her veins.

"That's my girl! It's going to be ok, I promise. Go to the mall and call me when you get back to the house. I will pick Jackson up from practice and we should be home around seven."

"Thank you, I will figure out something for dinner and see you then. I love you."

"I love you too baby. Call me if you need me." He said as he disconnected.

Liz decided right then she was done feeling sorry for herself. She had come through so much in her life. She was smart and strong, and she was not going to allow this to break her. This piece of shit wants to go to trial then that was fine with her she was going to make sure that jury sent him away for a long time. Liz threw on her gym shoes and grabbed her iPod and headed to the treadmill in the basement before she showered to go to the mall. After three miles of sweating it out to eighties rap, she pulled on Jackson's boxing gloves and began to swing at the punching bag Antoinne had bought him. It hurt her hands even with the gloves on, but it felt so good to hit something. She punched the bag over and over until her knuckles were throbbing and sweat was pouring down her face. She felt better than she had in weeks. Liz was taking back her power over her life starting today. She got in the shower, blew out her hair, put on some light makeup, jeans, ankle boots and black sweater and headed out the door.

When Liz got in the car, she was feeling much better. Before backing out of the garage she sent a text to Antoinne. "Did a few miles on the treadmill with Tone Loc and then beat the hell out of that punching bag, wow my hands hurt but I feel like a new woman, so don't worry about me, I am ok, and I love you. Xoxoxo" She hit send and then texted Caroline. "Going to the mall. The piece of shit is going to trial. I am going to Jamaica with Antoinne, meet me for lunch at Nordstrom at one?"

First text back was from Caroline "Jesus Christ. See you at one."

The second text was from Antoinne. "You are hitting it wrong, I will show you how to hit it tonight. Be careful world my baby is fragile. Not like a flower, like a bomb! xoxoxo"

Liz laughed out loud to herself and backed out of the driveway and drove the twenty minutes to the mall. She had an hour to kill before Caroline was meeting her, so she went to Macy's to hit the sale rack and find a few left-over summer items for her trip. She found two sundresses and a beach cover up that would be perfect. She still was hoping to find a new little black dress for one night there, but nothing was quite what she envisioned so she would have to keep looking. Lunch with her sister was just what she needed, and Liz was glad she had decided to call her. They talked about the trial and Caroline promised to be there by her side. She also agreed to keep Jackson while Liz and Antoinne went to Jamaica. It felt good to just vent. She was in a much better state of mind now than she had been when she first received the call this morning. Liz knew it would be one of the hardest things she ever did but like her sister reminded her she had to do everything in her power to make sure this piece of shit never had the chance to do this to another woman because the next one might not get out of it alive. There was no way Liz was going to take that chance, she would do what she could to get him locked up for as long as possible and every time he was up for parole, she would be there to remind the world of what he did to her and what would have happened if Antoinne not shown up when he did.

On the way home Liz stopped the grocery, she was going to make beef stew and homemade rolls for dinner, a little comfort food couldn't hurt. She threw the stew in a roaster and put it in the oven and set her bread dough on the warm stovetop to rise.

Chapter 16

The following Monday Liz dressed in her black dress pants and beige cashmere sweater headed out to meet with the Victims' Rights Advocate at the prompting of both Antoinne and the prosecutor's office. Liz figured they were right, and it was best to be totally prepared for what was going to happen the following week when the trial was expected to begin. Her stress level was growing exponentially by the day. She was trying her hardest to exercise, meditate and deep breathe but nothing seemed to be working, she just needed this trial to be over with soon. She was trying desperately to focus on the week following the trial when she and Antoinne would be in Jamaica putting this whole ugly mess behind them and enjoying the sun and the beach. Liz parked in a lot two blocks away from and walked to the court administration building. After going through security, the guard directed her to the second floor where the Victims' Rights Advocates had a small office. Liz for some reason pictured a room full of overweight, angry, lesbians with law degrees and a severe hatred toward anything with a penis. She did not want their help and she was not sure why she was there. She thought about leaving but she had promised Antoinne she would at least hear what they had to say so she was not too caught off guard when she was put on the stand. She hated that she was anyone's victim. She wanted to slap the sonofabitch who put her in this position, she actually wanted to castrate him, but she did not think the judge would allow it even though she would be doing society a huge favor. The world was completely unjust she thought, especially the fucked up legal system and she hated that she was a part of it even more. She entered the office with a chip on her shoulder and a wish for vigilantism to be legal. Much to her surprise there was a young, Hispanic man working as the receptionist. She gave him her name and he told her Ms. Cooper would be out to see her shortly. Liz flipped through a magazine trying to calm her nerves and talk herself into being nice. A few minutes later Ms. Cooper stepped into the room. Liz smiled to herself. She was exactly what Liz had been expecting. Ms. Cooper was over six feet tall. She weighed around three hundred pounds. She was wearing a long flowing skirt of multiple bright colors and a red sweater that was almost as long as the skirt. She wore a beret with long, grey, frizzy hair sticking out from under it in every direction. It was like looking back into the face of 1962. Liz somehow knew as she approached her to shake her hand that the scent of patchouli would invade her nostrils and stay there the rest of the day.

"Hello Ms. Bartlett, won't you please come in?"

"Thank you, Ms. Cooper," Liz said as she followed the mountainous woman down the hall. They walked into a small conference room that held a round table and four chairs and nothing else. Liz took a seat on the far side of the table. "I am not really sure why I am here Ms. Cooper" Liz stated flatly.

"Well basically I want to explain to you what will happen when you get to court. We have found that people tend to relax a little when they know what to expect, it's usually worse in their imaginations than in court.

"Ok, I appreciate that" Liz said, willing this meeting to go faster in her head and trying to be hostile since these people were really only trying to help.

"First of all, you will be in a room similar to this one for most of the trial, since you are testifying you cannot be in the courtroom until you get on the stand. The same applies to Mr. Fredericks, he will be secluded from you until you both testify. After that you will both be able to sit in the courtroom if you choose. I expect you will not be called until day two. The first day will be opening statements and law enforcement as well as forensics, which is basically the lab people verifying the DNA belongs to James Simmons. This is when the jurors will also hear from the physicians, the ambulance drivers, and the other professionals. Your testimony and Mr. Fredericks testimony will follow probably the second day if everything stays on track."

Liz sat quietly trying to take in everything that was being said. She just shook her head in understanding.

"Since the court does not want you or Mr. Fredericks talking and comparing stories, they will sequester you in different areas, you should both be testifying the same day so once you are done you can sit in the courtroom together. From what I understand the plan is for you to be the last witness so Mr. Fredericks will be in the courtroom when you testify because he will have already finished. Do you understand? Ms. Cooper asked very kindly.

"Yes, ma'am, thank you I do." Liz said quietly as she tried to process all the information that just thrown at her.

"Ok, now when you get on the stand the prosecutor will not ask you a lot of questions. They will simply ask you to tell the court everything that happened from the time you entered the house until you went to the hospital, in your own words, you will unfortunately have to relive the nightmare he put you through one last time. Try to keep it to the facts, try not to call your attacker any names or to swear. Just say it and be done with it." Liz shook her head in agreement. Now depending on how that goes and how the jury is reacting, the defense attorney is going to do one of two things. If he wants to get it over with and get you away from the jurors as quickly as possible, he will retain the right to recall you and ask you no questions. If he thinks that he can make you angry or he thinks that there is a chance, he can win over even one juror he will ask you some very intrusive and unacceptable questions. Most of them will be objected to by the prosecutor but he will try, and he may get a few of them through. He may ask you how many sexual partners you have had in your life. He may ask you if you have ever had sex on the first date. He may ask you if you were flirting with Mr. Simmons and what you were wearing." Liz felt her face grow hot as tears welled up in her eyes. She wanted to scream. She was attacked and now she was going to be on trial and this smug bastard would be watching her and terrorizing her and laughing at her while it happened. "Unfortunately, Ms. Bartlett, Mr. Simmons has more rights than you do, and this is how it works" Ms. Cooper said very matter of factly. Liz wanted to vomit. She stood quickly and thanked Ms. Cooper for her time and practically ran out of the office and down the hall to the elevator. She was breathing so hard by the time she got to the car she thought she might faint. She pulled out her phone and dialed Antoinne. When he answered she could not talk? Liz tried but she choked out a sob instead.

"Baby! What's wrong are you ok?" Antoinne was in a complete panic when he heard Liz crying unable to speak. "Sweetheart take a deep breath, please. Tell me what is happening!" Liz took a deep breath and was finally able to speak.

"I am at the court, I just met with the Advocate. She told me they are going to ask me things like how old I was when I lost my virginity and if I have ever had sex on the first date and if I was flirting with that mother fucker who attacked me!" Liz was crying so hard she couldn't say anymore.

"Hey stop crying! You are going to be ok. You have done nothing wrong and fuck them! We will get through this I promise. You cannot let this asshole win and when you allow this to upset you so much, he is winning!" Antoinne was grasping for words and Liz knew it. He did not know how to fix this and right now he was trying desperately to get her to calm down before she had to drive. He was kicking himself for not going with her. "I can come and get you right now and we'll just get your car later." Antoinne was already packing up his things to leave the office.

"No, no I am ok." Liz took a deep breath and hit the steering wheel. I am going to find a Starbucks and grab a cup of coffee, I will be ok, it just caught me off guard. I was not expecting to hear that I will really be the one on trial." Liz was trying hard to gather her composure.

"I don't want you to drive yet." Antoinne said firmly.

"I know, I am not." I am going to walk around the corner, I think I saw a Starbucks when I pulled into the lot." Liz told Antoinne.

"Ok, well I am going to stay on the phone with you while you walk there." Antoinne was not about to let her hang up until he knew she was ok.

"Ok well let's go then, I should hit a bar instead but right now if I start drinking, I am not going to stop." Liz was out of the car walking toward the area where she thought she saw the Starbucks.

She wiped her face on the sleeve of her sweater. She knew she looked like a hot mess, but she did not care. "Please tell me something good, I need a distraction." Liz begged Antoinne.

"Ok, well I was thinking when we go to Jamaica, we should make love in the sand on the beach under the moonlight. We'll sneak off to find a private spot where we can be alone. I want to take off all of your clothes and watch the breeze blow your hair and harden your nipples. Then I want to drop down on my knees in front of you and kiss every inch of your naked body."

"Wow, I am feeling much better now." Liz felt her face heat up, worried one of the customers in line may hear her conversation.

"Good because as soon as this is over that is my plan. I am going to make love to you all over that island. In our bed, in our shower, on our balcony, on the beach, in the water. I am going to take you again and again and I am never letting go."

It was everything Liz wanted to hear. "I love you Antoinne. I would be so lost without you. One venti, nonfat, no foam latte please" He began to laugh into the phone. "Sorry, I had to order my coffee!" Liz said knowing the mood was now kind of wrecked.

"Baby! I am trying to be smooth here and you are ordering coffee!" He teased Liz.

"I know and I cannot wait for our trip. Thank you" Liz said to the barista as she grabbed her cup and headed out the door back toward her car. "You are such a wonderful man, I don't know what I would do without you."

"Well you won't ever have to find out." Antoinne said in a deep and serious voice.

Liz reached the car and felt like a new person. "Thank you for talking me off the ceiling" She said gratefully.

"That is what I am here for" He responded without hesitation. They decided to just order pizza for dinner and Liz disconnected and headed toward home to get Jackson from practice. She felt completely and totally drained, and she knew this was a feeling she better get comfortable with for the next week of her life.

When Liz pulled up to practice, she walked up to the field to watch her boy, the season was wrapping up, they had their first playoff game on Saturday, if they won, they would play on Sunday and if they won that one then they would play for the district championship the following Saturday and then the season was over. Jackson would have a two week break before rugby workouts started. Liz worried he was too busy, but he seemed to love it. This was his last season before high school, she became instantly sad thinking about how short her time left with him was, he was growing up too fast. After practice ended Jackson grabbed his backpack and they headed to pick up the pizza. "How was practice?" Liz asked leaning across the front seat to kiss her boy on his sweaty cheek.

"Great, but I am starving!" He was always hungry.

"Well I ordered a couple pizza's so they should be ready, and you can eat as soon as we get home." Jackson spent the rest of the drive explaining their playoff schedule to Liz and reminding her of the extra practice Friday night. He was pretty confident they had a good chance of making it all the way to the district championship. Liz hoped he was right, she knew anything less would be heartbreaking for her son and she could really use the distraction right now too. Jackson showered, did his homework and headed to bed by nine. Antoinne was at her desk on his computer getting some work done. Liz poured herself a glass of wine and started the water filling the tub with bubbles. She turned on some soft music, lit a couple candles and slid out of her clothes into the steaming bath. She leaned back, shut her eyes and let the stress wash away. She heard the door knob turn and opened her eyes to see Antoinne standing naked before her. His lean, dark body was rock hard and perfect, she could not take her eyes off of him. His erection was huge. "Do you have room in there for me?" He asked coyly, smiling down at Liz.

"Oh, I think I can make room for you" Liz said as she slid over to one side. "No sit up, I am going to slide in behind you." He ordered.

Liz leaned into him and rested her back against his chest. He wrapped his arms around her rubbing the soapy water all over her breasts. She shut her eyes and enjoyed his touch. Antoinne kissed the back of her neck, sucking her skin. She felt his hardness against her. He reached across her hips between her legs and began to stroke her with his long, gentle fingers. Liz let out a soft moan. He knew exactly how to touch her. She arched her back and let him work her body magically, she felt every muscle in her body tighten. Faster and faster his fingers moved. Her legs began to shake in climax. "Oh God Baby" she moaned.

"Tell me you want it." He commanded.

"Give it to me, please. I need it." She whispered."

"Tell me what you want" He pleaded.

"I want you inside of me." Liz obeyed.

  He parted her legs with his, sliding himself directly under her, he lifted her hips and entered her from behind. Liz gasped. She gripped the sides of the tub for balance. He wrapped his hands around her wrists and held them firmly so she could not pull away. Antoinne's strong body moved harder and faster inside of Liz.

"Mmm. You belong to me" Antoinne moaned as he buried himself deep inside of her.

Antoinne grabbed Liz's shoulders and pulled her back hard against him, forcing her take all of him inside of her. Oh my God" she cried out. She was going to explode again. "Please don't stop, please. "she begged.

"Tell Daddy what you like." He insisted.

"Oh God, you feel so good. I like that, God you are huge." Liz tried to get the words out. The words she knew he liked to hear.

"Oh Baby" Antoinne cried as his hips thrust harder and harder, faster and faster. The water rocked with their bodies spilling over the sides of the tub. Liz couldn't catch her breath. He felt so good inside of her. Her body was made for him. Antoinne pulled back hard on her hips and exploded. Liz's shaking body collapsed back against him. He wrapped his arms around her and held her tight.

Chapter 17

Saturday morning Antoinne loaded a blanket and the stadium chairs into the back of Liz's SUV while she made a thermos of hot chocolate and packed a cooler of snacks for everyone, If Jackson's team won their game, they would play again the next day, it was now down to a one game elimination for the district championship. It was a sunny day, but the temperature was only expected to reach fifty degrees, so they were bundled up. Most of Liz's family was coming to cheer him on, which she knew he appreciated but it definitely added to his stress. Jackson had to be the field by noon for the two o'clock game. Antoinne had dropped him off and come back to pick up Liz. He was playing wide receiver today. Liz said a silent prayer to keep his feet swift and his body safe and climbed into the passenger seat. When they pulled into the parking lot Liz's sister Caroline and her husband George were there with their three youngest. Liz kissed her nieces and nephew and George grabbed the cooler. Antoinne had the stadium chairs and blankets, they looked more like they were headed out for a weekend camping trip than a football game. They found Liz's parents in the stands who also brought a cooler and blanket. Liz had told her dad the kids football games were alcohol free but apparently, he thought she must have been kidding because his thermos was filled with some sort of adult beverage which he swore was just medicinal to keep him from getting too cold. George and Antoinne both seemed surprised and amused by his explanation, but Liz and Caroline knew their dad too well to be shocked. About ten minutes later Jenna arrived, she too had a flask in her jean jacket. Liz worried they would all be thrown out by half time. Minutes later the announcer welcomed Jackson's team, the Bulldogs onto the field. Since they were the home team the stadium full of people were on their feet cheering for the boys. Jackson immediately spotted Liz and gave her a quick wave, it melted Liz's heart that he still did this, and she hoped it never stopped. As they approached halftime Jackson had scored one touchdown and his team was leading by fourteen. By the fourth quarter the gap had closed. The Bulldogs were up by a field goal with thirty seconds left. Jackson was defense, he was one of the fastest players on the team, so his coach put him in at Safety. Liz held tight to Antoinne's hand when the Mustangs snapped the ball and completed a twenty-yard pass to their receiver. He was headed straight to the end zone with only Jackson to stop him. Jackson ran as fast as his legs could carry him. The crowd was on their feet screaming, Liz wanted to turn away, but she couldn't. She saw her son closing the gap with fierce determination. Jackson went low and hit him hard at the fifteen-yard line. The ball went flying and was pounced on by one of Jackson's teammates. The crowd went wild! Jackson stopped the game winning touchdown. Antoinne and Liz screamed, she felt like she would burst with pride. The entire family was cheering and screaming when Jackson pointed to Liz and touched his heart. She did not know if she should laugh or cry, it was so sweet. Everyone around her laughed. He was quite the performer and loved the attention he was getting. "One game down, two to go!" Liz said leaning over to give Antoinne a quick peck. Her family and Jenna all agreed to meet at the next day for his next game. The location would not be determined until that night when they found out who they were playing. Whichever of the two teams has the best record would get the home field advantage. Liz told everyone she would send out a text that night. They all waited in the parking lot for Jackson to come out after the game to congratulate him. He was walking on air. "This" Liz thought to herself. "This is why I can take whatever comes at me because I have this amazing kid and this wonderful man, and I am the luckiest woman alive." She said a silent prayer of thanks and hugged her beautiful son. Everyone hugged and congratulated him and people all over the parking lot told him what a great job he did. He was smiling from ear to ear.

Sunday morning, they awoke to snow flurries and wind. Liz texted her parents and sister and Jenna and told them to all stay home, there was no point in everyone sitting there freezing for two hours, hopefully Jackson's team would win, and they could all come to the division finals the following Saturday. Jackson seemed a little disappointed that everyone was not coming but Liz told him he would just have to win so they could all see him play in the championship game. She pulled out his layers of under armor and an extra pair of socks to go under his game socks. Antoinne had bought hand warmers go inside his gloves and his cleats. He would still be cold but hopefully this would help keep him a little more comfortable. The team was having an early breakfast together at the high school so Antoinne dropped Jackson off while Liz showered and got ready. It was not unusual for there to be a little snow by this point in the season but today promised to be completely miserable with wind and snow so she and Antoinne would tough it out alone. Jacksons team had the home field advantage again. Despite the weather the stadium at was filled with people. Liz and Antoinne were surprised to see the high school marching band was there to play the local fight song and bring the team onto the field. It gave Liz a quick flash of what the next four years would be like on when Jackson was playing on Friday nights. Liz could not see his face under his helmet, but she knew her son was loving every minute of the excitement. They dominated the game with ease even in the snow. Jackson scored twice and the team was headed to the district championship the following Saturday. He was walking on cloud nine and so were Liz and Antoinne.

Chapter 18

The following Monday the trial began. Liz had tossed and turned all night and felt exhausted before she even had her coffee. Liz and Antoinne were not allowed in the courtroom today since they were testifying the next day. Caroline and Jenna and Liz's parents all decided to be in court for the whole trial. Liz told them it was not necessary, but they all wanted to be there and to make sure the jury saw Liz had a support system in place. Liz's dad also wanted to make sure the prosecutor did a good job. Liz convinced Antoinne to go to work, there was nothing they could do that day and there was no point in sitting in a small conference room alone waiting. The prosecutor had tried to insist that they did just in case there was a slim chance they would be called today. Liz promised they would keep their phones on and be there in an hour if necessary, but she was not going to sit in a little, windowless room all day watching the minutes tick by regardless of what they wanted. She decided to pack their suitcases for Jamaica. It was a good distraction and would help keep her mind off of what was happening. Antoinne hugged her hard and held on for a long time before taking her son to school. Jackson never really asked the Liz the details about her attack. She knew he had questioned Antoinne and he had been told she was beat up by a crazy man who came into the house they were working on. He did not elaborate and that seemed to be enough for Jackson, he told Antoinne that they better lock the bastard up and Antoinne assured him they would, without correcting his language. Liz had not wanted to talk about the trial or what was happening at the courthouse. Antoinne tiptoed around her and treated her like she might shatter into a million pieces any second. She felt angry and frustrated and on edge. She tried to keep herself busy all day. Liz tried to stay focused on the upcoming trip. The trial should finish the following afternoon and the prosecutor believed the jury would only deliberate a few hours at most and things should wrap up Wednesday afternoon. Caroline called Liz at lunch. She sounded drained, Liz hated that her family was there living through her horror, she knew it was upsetting them and it made her feel terrible. Caroline was quiet on the phone. Liz had been told to ask nothing about the trial, so she questioned her on how their parents were holding up. Caroline told her if their dad could get to him that it would save the state a lot of money because he would kill the piece of shit right then and there. Liz felt sick, she just needed this whole ordeal to be over with. She tried to convince her sister to get them to just leave and go home but she knew it was falling on deaf ears. After packing she spent an hour on the treadmill and then took a long hot shower. She made a cup of tea and packed Jackson's bag for the days he would spend at her sister's while they were in Jamaica. When she finished that task, she cleaned the house before she moved to the kitchen to make dinner, keeping herself busy was the only way she was going to make it through the day. Liz mixed bread dough, cinnamon rolls would thrill Jackson. She then started a big pot chicken soup. By the time Antoinne and Jackson got home she had more food than she knew what to do with, but she had kept her mind off of what was happening, what she would endure the next day and what her best friend and family were dealing with at the courthouse. Dinner was quiet. Jackson told them about the district championship game on Saturday, he would be playing both ways, Liz worried it would be too much, but it was the last game of the season and he could not be more thrilled. He was starting at wide receiver and would also be helping out at safety. She hoped they would win the game, it would be so hard to leave him for five days at her sister's if his heart was broken when they left. They were leaving early Sunday for Jamaica. She just needed to make it through the next few days. Antoinne helped Liz clean up the kitchen and then assisted Jackson with his math while she took another hot shower, she just kept trying to wash off the feelings that kept creeping up on her. The memories of the attack and how she would have to retell it to a room full of strangers in disgusting detail the next day were making her skin crawl. Liz threw on her pajamas and crawled into bed. Antoinne joined her about an hour later. Liz was grateful to feel his arms wrapped around her. Right now, she just needed to be held and did not want him to let go of her. Antoinne kissed her softly on the neck. "What can I do for you?" He asked so sweetly. "Just tell me I have the strength to make it through the next couple days. Tell me that it is going to be ok and that they will lock the sonofabitch up for a long time. I swear I don't know if I can do this, Baby." Liz felt the tears start to run down her cheeks. Antoinne took her shoulders and rolled her over so she was facing him. She wrapped her arms tight around his neck. He pulled her close against him.

"Listen to me. You are the strongest, bravest woman I have ever met. You are beautiful and smart, and you will not let this control you. I promise you, I will be there the whole time and I will do everything in my power to keep you safe for as long as I live." Antoinne was trying so hard to reassure her. He still blamed himself for the attack, she could hear the guilt in his voice.

"Antoinne you saved my life, and I owe you so much." She whispered in his ear.

"No, I should have been there, and I should have stopped it." He had tears in his eyes.

"You told me not to go! I should have listened. You kept him from killing me, and worse! Please baby, don't blame yourself.!" Liz was crying now too.

"Shh. This is almost over. We just need to get through the next couple of days and then we are going to spend five amazing nights on an island putting this behind us." He held her tight. She closed her eyes and fell asleep in the arms of the love of her life.

Liz slept hard. It was exactly what she needed. She woke up ready to fight. She put on a dark blue suit and cream-colored blouse. Antoinne was in a grey suit. They looked ready for battle. Liz tried to keep the morning light, she did not want Jackson upset and worried about her. After they dropped him at school they headed to the courthouse in Detroit, with rush hour in full swing it was going to take a full hour to get there. Antoinne drove and held Liz's hand the entire time. They were both very quiet in the car, Liz put her head back and shut her eyes and tried to think about their trip and not about how the day would unfold. When they arrived at the courthouse Antoinne was going to be testifying first, he hugged her hard and kissed her on her forehead, "You can do this, I will be right there, you look at me and you focus on me." Liz shook her head in agreement and watched him walk toward the courtroom. She was taken to a small conference room by one of the victims' rights advocates to sit and wait. She was able to take her Jamaica travel guide and a pad of paper with her so she thought she would try to make notes about their upcoming trip for her article. No electronics were allowed in the courthouse it had to be done the old-fashioned way, but it would keep her distracted while she waited to be called to the stand. After about an hour an officer came into the room and told Liz it was time. She felt her stomach tighten and immediately began to sweat. The officer was very kind. "You will do great Ms. Bartlett; just remember you did nothing wrong and all you have to do is tell the court what he did to you." Liz shook her head in agreement and followed the officer into the courtroom. The room had five benches on each side. There were about fifteen people scattered about, one was writing notes, Liz knew she had to be a reporter. Liz was immediately horrified at the thought of this making it into the paper and wanted to tell the woman to get out, but she knew she had to keep walking. She saw Antoinne and her family in the front row. As she passed them, he reached out and gave her hand a quick squeeze. Liz walked through the swinging gate, behind the officer and directly to the witness stand. She tried to keep her hand from shaking as she was sworn in. She saw the orange, jail issued jumpsuit out of the corner of her eye, but she could not look at the man who attacked her. The jury was to her right and the judge sat higher up on her left on a giant oak podium. There were more men than women on the jury. It was more black people than white people and the majority looked to be over forty. Liz tried to focus on Antoinne. He looked very upset. She could see his fists were clenched and his jaw was set tight. He locked eyes with her and gave her a nod, letting her know that she could do this. Liz took a deep breath as the prosecutor approached the stand.

"Good morning Ms. Bartlett, I am prosecuting attorney Megan Morrison, I need to ask you a few questions, I will try to keep this brief. I need you to tell the court in your own words what happened to you on June 24th. Liz took a deep breath and looked directly at Antoinne when she spoke. She spoke softly and told them all exactly what she remembered. She told them about the storm and how her attacker smelled of alcohol and how she tried to get out the back door and then the front, but he yanked her back inside by her hair and threw her to the ground. How he hit her so hard that her nose was broken, and blood was pouring out of her face and the back of her head. She told them how she kept picturing her little boy and how she fought with everything she had because he needed her. This is when her voice started to crack, and tears began to roll down her cheeks. She told them about how he was ripping her skirt off of her when Antoinne came in and rescued her. She could see her mother and sister were crying. Antoinne was so angry she could see him breathing very hard and deliberately, trying to stay calm. He nodded his head at Liz again, giving her all of his strength to keep going. Liz's dad got up and walked out of the courtroom. She hated putting them through this even more than herself. After Liz finished telling the prosecutor what happened she glanced at the jury to see two of women wiping tears from their eyes. The prosecutor then asked Liz if her attacker was in the courtroom and to please point him out. Now Liz had to look at him. She was shaking when she lifted her arms and looked at him and pointed to James Simmons. He stared directly at her with no emotion whatsoever. The defense attorney approached Liz. He saw the impact her statement made on the jury and now she knew he had to do damage control. Liz was not about to let him intimidate her. She hated the legal system and that applied to attorneys as much as criminals she thought it was so broken and backward, she never wanted to be a part of any of it and now here she was in this courtroom reliving the worst moments of her life for total strangers. She knew it had to be done. She knew it was up to her to make sure this piece of shit never did this to another woman, but she still hated every step of it. She stiffened her back and got ready for a fight.

"Liz, may I call you Liz?" He asked.

"Only if you want me to address you by your first name Barry." Liz responded curtly. She heard two of the juror chuckles. "I apologize, Ms. Bartlett. Is it true that the door was open and when Mr. Simmons came in you welcomed him and told him to take a look around?"

"Yes, it was an open house." Liz replied.

"Is it true that you flirted with Mr. Simmons in hopes that your boyfriend would show up and catch you and be jealous?" He asked casually. Liz felt her face turn bright red and tears start to fill her eyes.

"No! Look at him! He is disgusting and dirty and I would never, ever flirt with him! He attacked me." Liz was sobbing now.

Antoinne jumped to his feet. Liz saw Jenna grab his arm and pull him back down and said something to him to try and calm him down. The last thing any of them needed was for Antoinne to get in trouble with the judge.

"Is it true that you and Mr. Fredericks were broken up at the time the incident occurred? Liz looked at Antoinne, he just nodded his head at her letting her know she needed to keep going. "Yes." Is all that she responded.

"Ms. Bartlett have you ever had a one-night stand?" Liz was stunned. Her face turned red.

"Objection!" screamed the prosecutor. Antoinne was again on his feet.

"One of the court officers approached him and Liz could see that he was telling him if he stood up again, he would have to leave the courtroom.

"Withdrawn, no more questions at this time, your honor." The judge told Liz she may step down. She walked immediately out of the courtroom with Antoinne directly behind her. When they stepped into the lobby, he wrapped his arms around her, and Liz sobbed into his chest. She asked him to please just take her home. He thought she should be in the courtroom and hear the closing arguments after lunch. The jury needed to see her there. Liz finally agreed and went to find her a cup of coffee. When they returned Liz's, family was waiting in the hall outside of the courtroom. There was a one-hour break and then the closing arguments would begin. Her parents and sister and Jenna went to get a sandwich, Liz tried to persuade Antoinne to go with them, but he refused. She could not eat anything. They sat silently on a bench with his arm around her and her head on his shoulder. They were both drained and he was so angry he wanted to kill that bastard and Liz knew it. Finally, she spoke. "I am just thinking about how nice it is going to be to step off that plane and get to the beach and have a nice, tall drink. I cannot wait to see the ocean and listen to some good music and just relax."

"Me too, I am ready for this shitshow to be done with!"

"Thank you so much for everything, I don't know how I would have made it through any of this without you."

"I love you, I can't imagine being anywhere else." He stated matter of factly.

When they returned to the courtroom Liz sat between her sister and Antoinne, holding both of their hands. The prosecutor spoke first and went through every detail of the attack. She reminded the jury of every stitch on Liz's head and face, of her broken nose and ribs, of the pictures of all the blood. She told them that had it not been for Antoinne that they would probably being sitting here at a rape and murder trial or that Mr. Simmons would have gotten away to rape and murder other women. Liz cried. She tried so hard to stay strong but hearing it all again and thinking about what could have been, was just too much. The tears rolled down her face. Antoinne rubbed her arm and tried to comfort her but the more he heard the angrier he was getting. Liz was worried that if this went on much longer, he was going to grab James Simmons and his attorney and beat the living hell out of them. The prosecutor told the jury that Mr. Simmons clearly planned to rape and kill Liz and they needed to find him guilty of attempted murder.

The defense attorney stood to make his closing arguments and Liz felt Antoinne's hand tighten its grip on hers. He told the jury that Liz lead Mr. Simmons on, that she flirted with him and teased him and then when things started to go too far, she got scared. Liz was furious. She looked into the face of the jurors and she did not think they were buying into this bullshit. At least she hoped they weren't. Finally, the jury was given instructions and taken out of the courtroom. The judge suggested to both attorneys that everyone stick around for an hour, he thought they would come back with a verdict very quickly. The prosecutor seemed confident, but Liz was still nervous. She did not know what she would do if he was found not guilty and she did not know how she would keep Antoinne or her father from killing him if he was set free. They stood in the hallway where everyone tried to convince her that the jury was going to find him guilty very quickly and then this whole ordeal would be behind them. The minutes felt like hours. The judge had told the prosecutor that if they had not reached a decision by four that everyone would be sent home and they would reconvene at eight the next morning. She just needed this to be over, Liz did not know if she had the strength to come back the next morning. After an hour and twenty minutes the bailiff stepped into the hall to tell everyone to please return to their seats the jury had reached a verdict. Liz's family and Jenna walked in first. Antoinne turned to Liz and kissed her gently. "No matter what happens in there I am here and it's all going to be ok." Liz shook her head and put her hand in his and they walked back in to take their seats behind the prosecutor. The jury returned to the courtroom and Liz felt like they were all staring directly at her. They all stood as the judge returned to his place on the bench. The bailiff handed the judge the piece of paper from the jury and he read it and told James Simmons to stand. He turned to the jury and spoke. Liz felt the whole room start to spin. She couldn't catch her breath. Antoinne put his arm around her and whispered in her ear. "Hey, take a deep breath. It's ok. Don't fall apart on me now, it's almost over." Liz looked deep in his eyes and tried to focus on what he was saying and then she heard the word.

"Guilty." Liz's family let out a cheer and Liz began to cry. She looked at the jurors who were smiling at her and nodding in her direction. Liz mouthed "Thank you" to them. James Simmons showed no reaction. The judge thanked the jury for their service and set sentencing for December twenty first. They left the courtroom relieved and exhausted. Liz had already decided she would send a letter to the judge but that she would not be at the sentencing. When they left the courthouse, everyone hugged Liz and encouraged her to focus on her trip and putting this whole mess behind her. Antoinne and Liz's dad had walked away from the group and were conversing privately. Neither man was much of a talker, so Liz was surprised to them engaged in conversation by themselves. They were all coming to Jackson's game on Saturday and then to Liz's for dinner afterward. Jackson would go home with Caroline that night because Liz and Antoinne had a six am flight. Liz was ready to focus on the future and put this whole mess behind her.

Chapter 19

Friday night Liz grocery shopped for Saturday's dinner and Antoinne went to Jackson's practice. Since they would be gone most of the day, she was cooking a big pot of chili it could easily go in the crockpot while they were at the game. She was also making cornbread muffins and a few hot hor d'oeuvres. Liz grabbed a couple gallons of cider from the cider mill on the way home and started chopping onions and peppers for her chili. She used three kinds of meat, ground beef, ground turkey and chorizo. She was hoping to be having a celebratory victory dinner for Jackson after the game the next day. The district championship was being played at the University of Michigan stadium in downtown Ann Arbor, it was a huge thrill for the boys to be able to play at one of the biggest college stadiums in the country and it would be something Jackson would never forget. Liz turned on her amazon playlist and sang along to her favorite country music, something she did not get to do much of when Antoinne and Jackson were home since they did not love her choice in music genres. As she prepared the chili, she counted her blessings and thought about her future. Christmas was just around corner, and Liz wanted it to be perfect. When they returned from Jamaica it would only be a few days until Thanksgiving, which they're having at her sister's house. She was anxious to set up her tree and celebrate with Antoinne and Jackson and everyone she loved. Liz left the chili on the stove to simmer while she moved on to the appetizers. A couple of spicy dips and a cheese and cracker platter would go well with the chili. She had also picked up a dozen caramel apples for the kids. When everything was set, she packed a cooler for the game. She loaded in Styrofoam cups and pulled out two big thermoses she would fill in the morning with hot cider. She had two dozen cinnamon doughnuts and various kinds of pretzels and popcorn. Antoinne and Jackson came home with a bucket of chicken, mashed potatoes and biscuits. Liz thought briefly about the bathing suit she had packed for Jamaica and grabbed a wing and half a biscuit. Jackson was talking nonstop about the game. The team they were playing was from a town about twenty miles north of Ann Arbor, they were big farm boys and it was predicted to be an even match up. They had been watching game film at practice all week. Antoinne told Liz they were some big boys, and this would be a tough one, but Jackson did not seem worried, he was confident and as far as Liz was concerned that was half the battle. Antoinne and Jackson talked game strategy while Liz moved the chili to a crockpot and put it in the fridge for the next day. Once the dishes were done the Yahtzee game came out and they spent the evening having fun, it was exactly what they all needed.

The next day Jackson had to be to the University of Michigan field at eleven for the one o'clock game. He was excited and nervous. The temperature was not even going to hit fifty degrees, but the sun was shining so it was as good as they could hope for in November in Michigan. Playing at the University of Michigan "big house" in Ann Arbor definitely gave Jackson's team the home field advantage. The marching band from the high school was there performing before the game and again at halftime. People were tailgating all over the parking lot, it looked a lot more like a college game than a district game being played by thirteen-year old's. One thing was for sure people loved their football in this part of the country. It was in their blood and Liz was no different. They all wore their team colors of black and orange to support the boys, it was mostly a sea of black and orange hats and scarves since the temperature demanded heavy coats. Liz was imagining Jackson's face when he was on that field that morning doing warm ups. He was in a college locker room now dressing for his last little league game before moving up to high school. She wished she could just be there for five minutes to witness his excitement and couldn't wait to hear all about it when the game was over. Like she had done a million times before, Liz said a quiet prayer asking God to keep all the boys safe today before they unloaded and headed to the stands. Jenna and Liz's whole family were there. Liz wanted to get as close to the boys as she could. The headed for the fifty-yard line and managed to get seats in the second row. The crowd was tiny compared to a typical Saturday college game so there were only a couple sections of bleachers open on each side of the stadium all in the lower part of the bowl. It was still going to be the biggest crowd Jackson had ever played in front of before. All the little league and local high school teams showed up in their jerseys to support the team and watch the game. Liz loved her community. Ann Arbor was a great place to raise Jackson. They set up the stadium chairs and pulled out the blankets. Liz poured hot cider and Jenna and her dad pulled out flasks to warm it up for the adults. One of the high school choir girls sang the National Anthem, it gave Liz goose bumps, she did an amazing job. Liz stood there proudly watching her beautiful boy with one hand on his heart, and his helmet in his other she could see his big smile, she was beaming with pride and felt so good about where their lives were right now.

The boys took the field to receive the ball. Jackson was playing his usual position at wide receiver for offense and had told Liz he would be playing at safety on defense again today as well. She knew by the time the game was over he would be completely exhausted, but his adrenaline would get him through the next couple of hours. The quarterback, Jackson's close friend Joey, threw the ball fifteen yards hitting Jackson right in the numbers and they had the first down. This set the momentum in full swing and the two boys dominated the field for the first half scoring three touchdowns and holding their opponents the Eagles to one, thanks to Jackson's fast feet at safety. He was the star of the show today and they were all loving every minute of it. The second half of the game brought about a lot of changes and the Eagles had two players on Jackson. Liz could see his frustration. Antoinne told her the coach needed to change up the plays and move things around a little. She could tell he really wanted to be on the sidelines coaching. The first touchdown of the second half was scored by the Eagles. Their running back managed to slip right through Jackson's fingers and Liz could hear the coach giving him a pep talk on the sideline letting him know he needed to shake it off and keep going. They were not going to win this game if Jackson lost his confidence. Liz squeezed Antoinne's hand as tension mounted across the stadium. Jackson took the field as wide receiver. Liz stood up, Jackson looked to her and she gave him two thumbs up, hoping to boost his confidence and remind him she was there. He gave her a nod and took his position after the huddle. Joey snapped the ball the him and he was off and running. He broke free and was tearing down the field with the ball tucked under his arm, as fast as his legs could carry him. Liz, Antoinne and the entire crowd were on their feet screaming and cheering as headed toward the end zone. The closest player was more than ten yards behind him as he crossed into the end zone and once again there was a two-touchdown gap between the Bulldogs and the Eagles. Jackson turned and pointed to his mom. She pointed back and made a heart in the air with her fingers. "Ok, this really needs to stop, it makes him look soft!" Antoinne said laughing and shaking his head.

The Bulldogs scored the extra point and the score was now 28 to 14. This was all Jackson needed to keep him going for the rest of the game. He was unstoppable. He prevented two touchdowns at safety and forced the Eagles to two field goal attempts, only one of which was successful. Liz was so happy for him; his hard work and dedication was paying off. It was such a nice change to focus on something so wonderful and positive after the shitstorm she had just come through. Finally, the two-minute warning sounded, and the Bulldogs were now up by 17. The coach pulled the starting boys, including Jackson and Joey and the let the second-string boys take the field as the sideline celebrating began. Liz could not wait to hug her son. She was so proud of him, he had done an excellent job, it was too bad his own father was missing it, but she was so grateful Antoinne and her family were there to share this day with them. Antoinne could not be prouder of Jackson if he was his father. He was more of a dad to her son then Jackson had ever known before. This was the happiest Liz had ever been. Nothing felt greater than watching her child succeed. The bell sounded and game was over, the Bulldogs were the district champs and Jackson were headed to his Freshman team as a superstar. Antoinne hugged Liz and they all moved to the sidelines to hug the boys and celebrate.

After the game Jenna and the whole family came to Liz's house for chili. Jackson showered and then talked nonstop about every play of the game. He was so excited and so animated. Liz was proud of him and proud of how he talked about what they did as a team and not about what he did personally, it showed good character which was much more important than football. After dinner was over Liz's parents and Jenna left. Jackson was headed home with Caroline's family to spend the week. Liz hugged her boy hard. As much as she was looking forward to this trip, she would miss her son so much while she was gone. Antoinne walked him to the car to remind him to be on his best behavior and to make sure he stayed up on his school work while they were gone. She saw him give Jackson a big hug before he got into the car and it melted her heart. Liz began cleaning up the kitchen and Antoinne ran the vacuum and tidied the rest of the house, he knew Liz would be up all night before she would leave and go out of town with a single thing out of place. He appreciated her need to keep everything tidy and loved the home she had created for them.

Chapter 20

They arrived at the airport by 4:30 Sunday morning for their six o'clock flight. The terminal was crowded, and it took forty minutes to get through security. When they finally made it to the gate Liz swallowed a Xanax and drank her small coffee before they boarded. She flew all the time, but she never really got accustomed to it, the takeoff was the most difficult for her. Once they were level and assuming the turbulence were minimal, she would be fine but leaving the ground was nerve racking and the Xanax her doctor gave her certainly took the edge off. Antoinne did not mind flying at all, this was their first trip together and Liz was excited to have him all to herself for the next five days. He had upgraded their seats to first class to surprise her, she was thrilled no one else would be sitting next to them and they would have a little more room to relax, getting up at such an earlier hour combined with the medication pretty much guaranteed she would sleep until they arrived. They boarded the plane and sat in the very front row. He held her hand as they took off, it instantly calmed her and made her feel safer. Liz shut her eyes and put her head on his shoulder. They both woke up as the pilot announced they were getting ready to land in Montego Bay. Liz and Antoinne stared out at the beautiful water and landscape beneath them. It was a perfect day the pilot announced it was a wonderful eighty degrees and sunny. When got off the plane they gathered their luggage and headed for the shuttle. It was a small but comfortable bus that stopped at three of the Couple Resorts on the island. Antoinne wanted to take a private car but since this was a work trip Liz needed to be able to write about the shuttle service in her article. There were ten other couples on the bus, three of them were headed to the same resort they were, and the rest were split between the other two neighboring resorts. The bus stopped about thirty minutes into their almost two-hour ride at a small roadside stand that sold jerk chicken and beer. Antoinne bought beer but neither of them felt comfortable eating chicken from a roadside stand. Liz just had bottled water, she knew she still had Xanax in her system and shouldn't mix it with alcohol. The scenery was like nothing she had ever experienced. There was a gorgeous mix of both mountains and beaches and beautiful flowers everywhere she looked. There was also extreme poverty. Tiny shacks cluttered the landscape, with small, shoeless children playing in the streets and yards. They drove along the coast through small villages and shanty towns. Once the bus even had to stop for a herd of goats that would not get off the small road, the little farms had no fencing, so animals just wandered freely. Liz was snapping pictures out the window as they maneuvered the countryside. Antoinne was talking to other the other people on the bus. Two couples had vacationed at this resort previously and were telling him about the Dunn River Falls excursion. To their left the Caribbean's beautiful lapping water was breathtaking. Liz had never seen water so blue. There were visible reefs jutting from the sea with a backdrop of mountainous cliffs, she was trying hard to capture it in a photo but knew she could not do it justice. The bus pulled into the Couples San Souci resort first. Liz and Antoinne were anxious to get off the bus. Antoinne took their luggage from the driver and tipped him as Liz snapped photos of the resort which was built right into the cliffs. They checked in to their room, it was a beachfront suite on the second floor with a large balcony overlooking the Caribbean. Their suite was large with twelve inch, off white tile flooring, the bedroom, directly on the right had a king-sized bed it tastefully decorated with blue and white bedding and plantation shutters on the large double windows. Antoinne dropped their suitcases there. In the bathroom there was a large glass shower with dual heads for two and double sinks. To the right was a spacious living area with a large wood carved, painted white bar that held a stocked mini fridge. On the bar sat a silver bucket with a chilled bottle of champagne and tray of chocolate covered strawberries. The furnishings included a loveseat, two chairs, a small table and French doors onto the balcony. The balcony was almost as big as the living room, it had a sofa and two chaise lounge chairs and a small bistro set. The direct view of the beach was amazing. There were stucco walls on both sides giving them complete privacy. Liz stood taking in the amazing beauty all around her. For the first time in months she felt completely relaxed. Antoinne joined her with glasses of champagne for both of them. He kissed her softly, handing her the glass. "To a perfect vacation" he said as they toasted and sipped the cool drink while taking in the scenery and enjoying the breeze. They decided to put on their swimsuits and head to the beach for a few hours before dinner. First, they enjoyed the chocolate covered strawberries and the tray of crackers and cheese in the refrigerator. Liz threw on her bathing suit and covered it with a short, floral cotton sundress and flip flops. Antoinne put on swim trunks and a fitted white t shirt and his slide sandals. As they left the room Antoinne reached for Liz and they walked hand and hand through the sand enjoying the beautiful breeze and exploring the grounds. The resort was nestled amongst the cliffs with nothing else around as far as the eyes could see. They walked about a half mile before they were completely alone. They dropped their towels, Antoinne took off his t-shirt and Liz removed her sundress and they sauntered into the water, it was cool and refreshing. Liz playfully began to splash Antoinne. He grabbed her hands and yanked her down in the water with him. She laughed and wrapped her arms around his neck and kissed him softly. He pulled her into him and held her close. As Liz floated behind him with her arms around his neck Antoinne paddled them deeper into the blue sea until she was not able to touch the sandy bottom. She wrapped her legs around his waist and put her mouth to his neck sucking his warm, salty skin. Antoinne reached around her and untied her top of her swimsuit. Liz nervously glanced around to make sure they were still completely alone. He lifted her out of the water far enough to tease her nipples with his tongue. He fervently kissed her neck and chest, as he removed her swimsuit. Liz reached under the water and slid down his trunks and began to stroke his manhood. She wrapped her naked, wet body around his. His full lips kissed her urgently, as he drove his huge erection into her. The cool water gently rocked their bodies. Liz enfolded her arms tight around his broad, dark shoulders. She loved the way her milky skin looked against his smooth, brown muscles. "God you are so beautiful." He moaned as he pushed her wet hair off her face and continued to move his hips into hers. Liz rode his body with ease, wave after wave, she loved the way he felt inside of her and ached for him when he wasn't there. "You feel so good, please don't stop." Liz begged.

"I want to live between your legs." He whispered. His unyielding hardness took her breath away. Antoinne kissed her urgently as he gripped her ass firmly and pulled her firmly down to take all of him. Liz felt dizzy as her climax built. She dug her nails into his back and bit his shoulder. "Oh God. Oh Antoinne." She moaned.

"Take it baby" He commanded. Faster and faster their hips moved together.

"Now. Please now." Liz begged. Antoinne succumbed to her command and erupted inside of her, Liz shuddered in orgasm and collapsed against him. Nothing in her life had ever compared to what she shared with this man, and she knew nothing ever would again. Liz was happier than she ever imagined she could be, and she prayed it would never end. They slipped their suits back on and walked hand in hand back to the beach. Liz was starving. They stopped at the poolside bar and ordered and couple drinks and a dozen jerk chicken wings. There was a band playing reggae music and several people were dancing. "Clearly the drinking starts early here" Liz commented as they watched the couples on the dance floor struggle to keep with the beat of the music. Antoinne joined a group of men playing beach volleyball and Liz relaxed in a chaise lounge chair and listened to the music while she watched them play. It was a perfect day. The sun started to dip into the horizon they left the pool area and went back to the room to get ready for dinner. Their reservation was for seven. Liz pulled two bottles of water out of the fridge and started the shower. They stripped out of their sandy suits and into the cool shower together. Liz ordered Antoinne to stay on his own side of the shower or she knew they would never make it to dinner. He laughed but did as he was told. She dressed in a long red maxi dress with strappy sandals and large gold hoop earrings. He wore a beige linen slacks and short sleeve white silk shirt. He looked so sexy she was not sure she could keep her hands off of him. "Wow you look beautiful" He said kissing her neck as he stepped up to the sink next to her to put on his cologne.
"Thank you, you look pretty good yourself." She said winking at him.
"Are you ready?" He asked looking her up and down.
"Yes, let's go." Liz put her hand through his arm, and they walked toward the restaurant. They dined indoors at the Casanova restaurant. It was understated and simple with tray ceilings made of wood and light-yellow walls. The waiter sat them along the bank of windows with a view of the beach, which was lit with lanterns as far as the eye could see. They ordered Caribbean crab cakes to start and for dinner Antoinne had the grilled rack of lamb and Liz decided on the catch of the day. They shared a bottle of wine and talked about their plans for the next day. They were getting up early to go snorkeling on a chartered sailboat and then they were having a private dinner on the beach. After their meal they headed down to the beachside bar where there was another band of musicians accompanying a beautiful young woman with a sultry voice. Antoinne found them a small table for two next to the dance floor. Liz dropped her bag and her wrap on her chair, and he led them to the dance floor. There was a cool breeze blowing in from the water, the night sky glittered with stars above them. It was dimly lit with lanterns along the edge of the dance floor and stage lights on the band. Liz put her arms around Antoinne's neck. He took her hips in his hands and guided her body with his to gentle rhythm of the easy island music. They talked to couples from all over the world. It was easy to make friends in such a relaxed atmosphere. Everyone laughed and danced, and Liz could not remember the last time she had so much fun. They met a couple in their forties from New Jersey named Vinnie and Gina, they were practically a walking sitcom. Vinnie told them how they spent the day exploring the nude beach that was located on the far side of the resort. Liz had read about it but had no intentions of visiting it and would only touch on the fact that the resort had one in her article. She had assumed that this area was frequented by more Europeans than Americans as nude beaches tended to be more commonplace in that part of the world. They told them of the horrors of seeing people naked and had them all laughing hysterically. Finally, at midnight they said goodnight to their new friends and walked back to the room. Liz slipped out of her dress and

into a black silk, short nightgown and matching robe. Antoinne was relaxing on the sofa on the balcony listening to the water crash against the shore when she walked out to join him. 'Come sit with me beautiful." He said patting the spot next him. Liz snuggled into his chest and wrapped her arms around his waist. "I did not realize how much I needed this vacation" He said stroking her hair. "We have been through so much the last few months, it feels good to just relax, without a care in the world." Liz replied.

She reached between his legs and began rubbing him through his clothing. She felt him stiffen immediately. Liz unzipped his pants and freed him from the confines of his underwear. She needed to show him again how much he meant to her. She leaned down and kissed his strong stomach and licked his hairline. Liz parted her lips and slowly took him into her warm, wet mouth. Antoinne moved her hair to the side and stroked her cheek as he watched her take him deeper and deeper. He moaned softly and gently rocked his hips. "Oh God Baby" He loved the sucking sounds she made. He played with her hair and encouraged her take more of him. Liz enjoyed having total control of his body, without taking her mouth off of him she slid off the sofa and directly between his legs. Antoinne grabbed her wrists firmly holding them at his sides, forcing her to use only her lips to please him. For a moment she let him slide out of her mouth and rub himself on her face, he loved the contrast of her porcelain skin against his. She teased him with her tongue before she let him thrust himself back to the sweet comfort between her lips. Liz gripped him with her mouth sucking hard, sliding him in and out, willing his juices from his body. "Oh my God "she felt his muscles tighten as he wrapped his hands in her hair and pulled her against him, he began to shake as she sucked harder and harder until finally, he exploded in her throat.

Liz slid back onto the couch next to him. Antoinne, still barely able to breathe wrapped his arm around her. "Woman, never, ever in my life. Wow. Oh my God."

Liz laughed and hugged him. "Well in case you don't realize it, I own you now." She said jokingly.

"Yes, ma'am you do. My God baby where did you learn to do that?!" He demanded. He was in awe of her skills and appreciated her beyond words but at the same time annoyed by her abilities to please a man in such a way. Liz smacked him playfully and replied, "I read a lot of books and don't act like that is the first time I have ever done that for you!"

"You have, but never like that!" He replied teasingly.

She grabbed his hands and pulled him up and lead them to bed.

Chapter 21

The next morning, they had breakfast delivered to their room early. The waiter set it up on the balcony so they could enjoy the views while they ate. Liz poured herself a big cup of coffee and stared out at the water. "Good morning" Antoinne whispered in her ear as he wrapped his arms around her and kissed her neck.

"Hey, did you sleep good?" She asked.

"Are you kidding me? Between the sea air and what you did to me? I slept like a baby!" Liz laughed and handed him a glass of orange juice. "I loved it, but I am still mad you know how to do that" He teased.

"I told you, I read a lot besides I have done that to your hundreds of times!" Liz joked back with him.

"No, not like that you haven't.!" Liz smiled and refilled her coffee cup.

She had yogurt and fresh fruit for breakfast while Antoinne had scrambled eggs, bacon and toast. After they finished breakfast they showered together and dressed for their catamaran excursion. They had booked a private tour guide to take them by sailboat around the island. The resort offered sunset cruises, but this was a chance to see the island by themselves and a good opportunity for Liz to come up with something new and innovative for her article. A shuttle transported them to the charter boat. Their tour guide Winston welcomed them aboard with rum punch. There was reggae music pumping through the sound system. Liz had Antoinne lather her with sunscreen before the boat pulled out into the azure waters. They cruised along the coastline and into the reefs where they were, they stopped to snorkel. Winston fitted them with masks, fins and life jackets before they jumped off the side of the and into the cool water. Liz was nervous but Antoinne stayed close to her and they saw amazing sites. The coral was vibrant, they observed fish all around, angel fish, seahorses, dart fish, butterfly fish and clown fish. Antoinne was able to capture the amazing views with their underwater camera. The coral was like nothing they had ever seen, purple base anemone mixed with red cauliflower coral and sun coral and teal coral. Liz had never snorkeled before and was in awe. She knew they would have to plan another trip for Jackson to experience such a wonder. After snorkeling they enjoyed another glass of rum punch as the boat traveled to a private location that Winston had assured them, they would love. They pulled into a small dock at an inlet that was hidden in the between the mountains. It was lush and tropical. Winston told Antoinne to follow the trail and it would lead them to a magnificent waterfall with a private swimming area and that they could enjoy the next two hours in this discreet paradise. She grabbed their beach bag and his hand, and they began to navigate the path. Liz was taking in the sounds and the smells as well as the sites. The air was salty but permeated with tropical flowers. There were beautiful birds flying all around them, after a mile hike they reached their destination. There was a small beautiful lake with a giant waterfall cascading into it off a fifty-foot cliff. It took her breath away. They both stopped in their tracks to take in the amazing beauty. Liz wrapped her arms around Antoinne's waist, she could not imagine being any happier than she was at the moment.

"This is so incredible, I couldn't be happier, and I love you so much, thank you so much for this."

"I feel the same way Baby, and I love you too." He said kissing her on her forehead. They dropped their beach bag and headed toward the water. It was an exquisite blue green and they could see to the bottom. The waterfall was coming from the mountains, so the water was cooler than either of them had expected, Liz let out a gasp when it hit her shoulders. "Wow that's cold!" Liz said shocked.

"Come over here" Antoinne said motioning her toward him. He moved to the edge of the streaming water and showed Liz where they could go in behind the falls. Liz took his hand and followed his lead. The area behind the falls was completely private. "Kiss me" He said pulling her close to him. His soft, full lips brush against hers. He slid his tongue into her mouth and sent shockwaves through her body. "This water is so cold! C'mon let's go over there under the tree and relax. Liz pulled their towels out and put them together to make a blanket on the shore of the lake. They laid down side by side looking up at the waterfall and mountains all around them. The blue sky cut through the thick trees and reflected off the water like glitter. "Stand up and take off your suit for me."

Liz shook her head. "No way, what if someone shows up?" Liz protested.

"Then I will cover you with my body, I promise." He smiled.

She hated to tell him no so Liz stood up and removed her swimsuit and laid down on the towel next to him completely naked. Antoinne pulled off his trunks and sat next to her. Looking down at her he ran his dark hands over her soft pink skin. His fingers traced her nipples as he admired every inch of her. Antoinne laid on top of her and kissed her mouth softly. He kissed her neck and sucked her nipples as he worked his way down her stomach. Liz loved his full lips on her skin. Antoinne kissed her hips working his way toward her center. Liz tried to protest, she worried someone would walk up and see them in this intimate situation. He positioned himself between her legs and held her hands down so she could not protest. He kissed her thighs. Liz let out a soft moan and spread her legs, she couldn't fight it she was eager for his mouth. Finally, he gave her what she needed. She felt his tongue slide into her. Liz arched her back, begging him not to stop. Over and over his tongue lapped her, circling and darting and licking until she lost control. As her back lifted off the ground he thrust his hardness inside of her. "Oh God" she screamed. Liz dug her nails into his back and held on to him. Antoinne slid deep inside of her wetness. "You feel so good." He moaned in her ear. "This is mine, do you hear me?" He asked in a commanding tone.

"Yes, I belong to you." Liz said, knowing that he liked to hear her say it, but she meant it. She belonged to him, body and soul. She loved him with every fiber of being, like she had never loved anyone before. Her hips moved to take him deeper inside.

"You are so beautiful, I love you baby." He said kissing her passionately. Their bodies moved together in perfect rhythm. When they finished making love Antoinne took her hand and led them back into the cool water to rinse off before they dressed and returned to the boat.

Winston greeted them on the dock. The smile on his face suggested he knew what they had been doing and Liz blushed as she walked past him. The boat continued along the coast, their guide pointed to landmarks along the ride back toward the pier. When they returned to the hotel the showered to get the sand and sex off their bodies, Antoinne told Liz when they got home, he wanted to have a double shower put in her bathroom so they could shower together every day. Liz laughed and told him no way. After the shower they crawled naked into bed to sleep off the afternoon sun, sex and rum punch.

Chapter 22

When Liz woke up, she was all alone. She called for Antoinne but there was no response. Liz put on her robe and walked into the living room. She found a note from Antoinne. "Planning something special for tonight. You have a massage at three and a hair appointment at four. See you after that, put on something beautiful. Xoxo. Love you." Liz threw on a pair of shorts and a t shirt and slipped on her flip flops before heading over to the spa. They gave her a full body massage with a sea salt scrub. Liz felt completely relaxed and loved the coconut and floral smell the oil left on her skin. The hairdresser gave her a trim and washed and blew out her hair, she went ahead and let them do her makeup as well. She left the spa feeling beautiful. When she returned to the room Antoinne had come and gone again and left another note. This one said he would return in thirty minutes and she should be ready for dinner. Liz only needed to get dressed. She decided on the new little black dress. It was a low cut A-line with a two-inch ruffle along the bottom and a cap sleeve. She put on a gold necklace with a three-inch abalone slide to give her a pop of color. She wore matching earrings and black wedge sandals. The massage oil left her skin with a beautiful shine, she felt good and was excited for their evening together. The hotel had a small beachfront area where they set up about twenty-five tables for waterfront dining. There were candles and lanterns surrounding the area and the brochures made it look like the most romantic place she could ever imagine having dinner. A few minutes later Antoinne showed up. "Hey where have you been? I missed you." Liz asked.

"I needed to go to the business center for a conference call, we had an issue at work, and I thought since I had to do that you might enjoy a little pampering, and clearly I was right because you look beautiful." Antoinne said looking her up and down.

"Well thank you kind Sir." Liz appreciated his attention.

"I just need fifteen minutes and I will be ready to go." he commented.

"Ok go ahead, I am going to step out on the balcony and give Jackson a quick call."

"Sounds good babe." He said walking toward the shower.

Liz called Jackson, she was so happy to hear his voice. "Hi Sweetheart, it's Mom."

"Hi Mom! How is Jamaica?" Jackson sounded happy to hear her voice.

"It's great, we went snorkeling today, you would have loved it, we are going to have to plan another trip so you can try it."

"That sounds great Mom. Is Antoinne having fun?"

"Yeah sweetie we are both having a great time, I miss you."

"I miss you too mom, but I am having lots of fun at Aunt Caroline's and Uncle George helped me with my math, so I got my homework done and Friday night we are going to the movie"

'That sounds great honey. I am so glad you are having fun. We will be home Saturday, I love you." Her heart ached a little.

"Love you too mom, see you Saturday." Jackson said as he disconnected.

It made it easier for Liz to relax and just enjoy her time with Antoinne knowing her son was doing well and having fun.

Antoinne emerged from the bedroom showered dressed in a beautiful pair of black pants and ivory linen shirt that looked amazing against his chocolate skin.

"Wow you look great, maybe we should stay in" Liz suggested as she walked closer to kiss him.

"Mmmm, you smell good too." She was becoming aroused just standing close to him.

"C'mon woman lets go to dinner before you start something, and I end up starving to death!" He teased, taking her hand and pulling her toward the door. Antoinne lead them down the sidewalk and past the beachfront restaurant. "I thought we were eating here tonight?" Liz asked as they continued at a pretty fast pace.

"Change in plans, I have a surprise." Antoinne said casually, pulling her along. They followed the long sidewalk, passed the main building, restaurants and pools and up a flight of stairs built into the cliffs. Liz wanted to ask where they were going but instead, she decided to just let him surprise her, this is obviously what he had been up to all afternoon and she felt so touched that he would go to all this trouble to make their night even more special. They climbed another set of stairs and finally arrived at a small gazebo on top of the cliffs jutting out over the water. It was decorated with iron torches around the perimeter, a white candle in the center of the table and small white lights wrapped around the gazebo posts. The table was draped in white linens with silver stemware and crystal champagne flutes. It was simple and elegant. There was a waiter there to serve them and an acoustic guitar play sitting on a chair about fifteen feet from the gazebo. It was the most romantic thing Liz had ever seen. Liz turned to Antoinne and kissed him softly. "It's perfect, thank you." No one had ever done anything like this for her before. Liz was stunned at the amount of effort he went through to make everything perfect. She could not imagine loving any man more than she love Antoinne. There was a shrimp appetizer waiting for them, the waiter poured them each a glass of champagne when they sat down. They looked out over the water and watched the sunset. The sky was beautiful shades of pink and gold and blue. The tide was coming in and the waves were crashing against the beach below them. The guitar was playing softly behind them while a gentle breeze blew. Antoinne took her hand and lifted her to her feet, he pulled her close to him and held her as their bodies moved gently to the music. Liz had never been more in love in her life. The thought of losing him terrified her and she quickly pushed it from her head.

The waiters approached carrying covered silver serving dishes and they sat back down anxious to taste the amazing cuisine.

"It's fantastic, I was starving." Antoinne commented taking another bite of his lobster. He poured them more champagne. They laughed and enjoyed the meal, Antoinne told Liz how he would like to plan another trip to a different island for mid-winter that included Jackson, they both knew he would love to try snorkeling. When they finished dinner Antoinne pulled Liz to her feet again to dance with him. She slid her body tight against his as they swayed to the easy music. When the song ended Antoinne whispered in Liz's ear. The surprises aren't over yet. We have to go.

Liz was enjoying their private dinner so much she hated to leave but she was excited to see what was next. Antoinne took her hand and lead her back to the beach where Winston was waiting with a boat. She knew Antoinne must have arranged this when they had gone snorkeling. Liz was overwhelmed with emotion and felt like she might cry. When they got on the boat Winston greeted them with more champagne. "Ok all this champagne is making me a little light headed." Liz whispered in Antoinne's ear.

"That's ok baby, I got you, just enjoy." He said kissing her softly. Their cruise was a slow ride around the lagoon. Soft island music played in the background. The boat dropped anchor about a half mile from the resort. Liz wondered what was happening. "I am not going skinny dipping in front of Winston and the guy driving the boat in the dark Antoinne!" Liz exclaimed.

Antoinne burst out laughing. "Baby do you really think I am gonna try and get you naked in front of these men? My goodness woman!" He was shaking his head at her when the sky exploded. Liz jumped, looking up to see fireworks. "Winston told me they had fireworks tonight over the bay, and I thought this would be a great way to see them." He was still laughing at her for thinking he was taking her skinny dipping with strangers. Antoinne wrapped his arms around her and pulled her close. They watched the beautiful show in the sky as the boat gently rocked. Antoinne turned to Liz and took her face in his hands.

"Liz, you are the love of my life. You make me crazy on every single level. I think about you when I am not with you. I cannot imagine my life without you. I love Jackson like he were my own son." He was getting choked up talking to her and Liz started to cry.

"I love you too. You have given me everything I have ever dreamed of and never thought I would have." Liz kissed him passionately.

Antoinne dropped to his knee in front of her. Liz gasped and put her hand over mouth. Antoinne's eyes filled with tears. "I don't ever want to live without you. Will you marry me?"

Liz started to cry. Antoinne pulled a ring out his pocket and presented it to her. It was a vintage two karat oval diamond surrounded by smaller stones, set in white gold. Liz gasped. "Yes of course I will marry you!" Liz cried holding out her hand for him to put the ring on her finger. Winston and the boat driver let out a cheer. Antoinne placed the ring on her hand and pulled her to her feet. He wrapped his arms around her and kissed her passionately. Liz had tears running down her face. "We have to call Jackson!" She exclaimed.

"He already knows, and he is thrilled. I asked him and your dad for their blessings before we left." Antoinne told her. Liz hugged him again. She had never been so happy in her life. The boat began its journey back to the resort and Liz snuggled into Antoinne and stared at her beautiful ring. Never in her life did she think she would have something so exquisite of her own. She had no idea this kind of happiness even existed.

"Let's get married this winter in St. Thomas, what do you think?" He asked as they were walking back to their room.

"I think that sounds perfect." Liz replied, kissing her fiancé.

Printed in Great Britain
by Amazon

21278734R00055